STAY ALIVE

CRASH

JOSEPH MONNINGER

SCHOLASTIC INC.

With love to my two Campfire Girls, Joan and Cathy
– JM

No part of this publication may be reproduced, stored in a retrieval system, or transmitted in any form or by any means, electronic, mechanical, photocopying, recording, or otherwise, without written permission of the publisher. For information regarding permission, write to Scholastic Inc., Attention: Permissions Department, 557 Broadway, New York, NY 10012.

ISBN 978-0-545-56348-2

12 11 10 9 8 7 6 5 4 3 2 1   14 15 16 17 18/0

Printed in the U.S.A.   40
First printing, January 2014

PART ONE

SURVIVAL TIP #1

Whenever you are lost, follow any body of water downstream. If you come to a lake, find its outlet and then follow it. Do not veer away from the water. Towns and cities — in fact, all settlements — are built beside water, and eventually a stream will bring you to some form of civilization. Civilization means help and rescue.

CHAPTER 1

Before the plane crashed, before it became more than the sound of a mosquito up in the sky, a moose, a great northern Alaskan moose, stepped into the bright body of water called Long Lake. The moose appeared coated in copper; he had been rolling in dirt and mud to rid his ears and body of the mosquitoes that peppered him all day. He weighed thirteen hundred pounds and stood over seven feet high at the shoulder. He possessed a forty-inch-long leg and measured ten feet from tail to nose. As distant relatives, he counted the wapiti or North American elk, the caribou, the mule deer, and the whitetail in his family. He was a deer, the largest in the world, and on this summer evening, his pedicels – two small knots of soft tissue just forward of the ears – had pushed out into what became, over the long summer season, the trademark symbol of moose: palmate antlers.

He was the first animal to notice the plane.

The sound of the plane changed when it was still a fair distance away from Long Lake. What had been a steady hum suddenly became erratic and choked. Gradually, as if the engine had tried to clear its throat and failed, the plane began to glide and spin. In all the world below, at least from the height of the plane, it seemed the only thing in motion. That was an illusion, of course, because the land beneath the plane teemed with life: the getting and keeping of calories, the squirrel on the branch, the jay, the Arctic char tucked under a white stone in cold, cold water. A cinnamon-colored bear, a grizzly, raked its fierce claws through a rotted birch log, the log cadaverous and round. The bear's eyes cast up for a moment at the spectacle of a silver creature falling, falling, falling. The bear went back to feeding, its front teeth snapping yellow, meaty grubs like popcorn kernels.

Δ   Δ   Δ

The plane dropped from the Alaskan sky in the last light of a late-summer evening. Seen from a distance, the plane's plummet might have contained an element of beauty. The dying sunlight flashed on its outstretched wings, and the sudden cessation of sound – the stalled engine, the slice of air over the fuselage, the creak of the wings' guy wires – signified the return of the natural silence that marked the north country. Wind canted the plane slightly to starboard, and if it were possible to be above the plane, one might have witnessed a flash of light coming off the pilot's window as the forward momentum of the plane began to slow.

The pilot thumbed at the radio, tried to restart the engine, looked hurriedly about him. Russell Hedgeman, fifty-four, had been a bush pilot for over twenty years, and he was competent and smart, a veteran, a fellow who had thrown his hat into the Alaskan guiding business years before. Two days earlier, he had already ferried *Junior Action News Team*'s film crew to the town of Takalut to scout locations on the southern slope of the Brooks Range. In other words, he did not panic. He had been in tight spots previously, but this time, with the plane fighting him, he felt a quiet enter his body and a premonition – yes, today was the day that he had waited for and fought off for a million miles or more – that he would not survive. Now that it was here, he did not mind it so much. He went through the necessary procedures, and if a pilot licensing board had recorded his actions, he would have passed their inspection, received nods of propriety. He did his best, and his best was quite good.

Russell Hedgeman aimed the plane as well as he could toward water. It was his only chance, the plane's best bet. He felt the steering harness in his shoulders and chest, and he yanked hard to get the plane to respond, but it was done listening to him. It had become a heavy, unresponsive thing, its shrug at giving in to gravity fierce and terrifying. It dropped nosefirst, and though Russell tried to get the nose to rise, the weight of the engine forced it down. In his last moments, Russell thought of a balsa glider he had owned as a boy: the lovely broad wings, the way he had once climbed to the top of a shady maple and launched the plane. It had flown for what seemed like miles on the North Carolina breeze, falling as softly as a leaf, the metal nose clip keeping the yaw intact, and once, on a stronger breeze, it had risen again almost to his height in the tree. A monumental flight. That's what Russell remembered as he felt the trees begin ripping at the plane's wings, the spars jabbing through and trying to impale him.

Eleven passengers falling from the sky. Nine *Junior Action News Team* members, the crew of a teen-based TV magazine show that brought the viewers different adventures from around the world. They were on their way to record a program near the Brooks Range in central Alaska about summer training for the Iditarod dogsled race. Four boys, one accompanied by his father. Three girls, one on the verge of international fame, two of them twins. One thirty-three-year-old producer: a short, gabby man who hated flying, hated kids pretty much, and thought his services would be better suited to working with a real television program, not some ridiculous preteen after-school show like *Junior Action News Team*.

The pilot, Russell Hedgeman, made ten. He did not see the branch that came through the window and ended his days at the cockpit.

The eleventh passenger – Buford, a four-year-old basset hound who was the *Junior Action News Team* mascot and had appeared on every show to date – rested in his crate inside the cargo hold. When the plane attained maximum speed in its spin to the earth, his ears flapped behind him like two scarves stapled to his skull. He tried to stand and howl, but the violence of the plane's passing through the treetops jerked him to the front of the crate, then the rear, then the side. He resembled a single die shaken in a cup and rattled forcefully in preparation of a throw onto a game board. Except in this case there was no game board.

The plane skidded to a stop in ten feet of water, the broken tail scraping on the bottom like an anchor thrown out to hook anything solid, and something cracked along the right wing and turned the plane like a lazy Susan. Water began rushing into the plane from every conceivable direction, and Buford, his nose sharper than that of any of the humans on the plane, smelled fish and grass and moose and bear and a thousand other scents he hardly recognized.

Then – before the screaming, the crying, the calls for help began – a moment of silence descended over the plane. Each ear turned to hear what would happen next, but there was no "next," unless you counted the slow weight of water creeping quietly onto the plane. For an instant, the tremendous wrenching of the plane exploded outward in waves of sound, but the echo returned back from the woods and bright water in silence. It was as if the natural world had accepted the sound, refined it, and returned it to each ear as a thread of silence.

Then at last, chaos.

CHAPTER 2

"Get the door open!" someone screamed.

But where was the door? Suryadi Thul looked at the EXIT sign beside him, then at the blood on his hand, then again at the EXIT sign. Someone behind him yelled over and over to get the door open, and he sensed perhaps it might be his responsibility because he sat next to the door, but he couldn't be certain it was *this* door they wanted open. It wasn't as if any of the team had said much to him up to this point. A new guest kid appeared on *Junior Action News Team* every week, and Suryadi understood he had been invited to play that role because he was Indonesian and would serve as a newcomer on the adventure they had planned. Given all that, he didn't feel exactly part of the group.

Besides, for the moment he was more interested in his own blood.

And water.

Water had come into the cabin, and he could not be certain, but he was fairly sure that if he opened the door, more water would rush inside. And that was not good. The plane sat on a 30-percent incline – Suryadi loved math and geometry and could not prevent his mind from doing the calculations, always calculations, that life presented to him – and the door was on the down side of the plane. What they needed to do, he thought, was exit from the up side of the plane, but he could not quite get his mind to work in an orderly fashion. Everything happened at once, and the blood on his hand shone red and shiny in the yellow glow of the emergency lights that had come on along the floor. He touched his hand to his head again, and he felt the warmth of his blood spilling out and would have given anything for a mirror in that moment, but that wasn't going to happen, he knew.

"Get the door open! Now! Get it open!"

He wished whoever it was would stop screaming so much.

The voice belonged to Walter Eliot. He stood nearly sideways, his hand up on the baggage compartment of the small plane to brace himself, his face wild and red and terrified. He could not swim. It was a lifelong embarrassment and a lifelong fear, and the sight of the water – the feeling of it creeping along the floor, growing higher by the instant – had made him nearly crazy with terror. A small part of his brain understood he was an adult among young people, that his own son watched him with wide-eyed amazement, but he could not help himself. He panicked. Somewhere, somehow, some time ago, someone had said something about life vests, but he had blocked out the information because he had no intention of going into the water, ever.

But now the water came toward him. Had found him after all this time. And so he stood, his body nearly sideways in the fuselage, and screamed over and over, "Open the door! Get the door open! Open it!"

The plane shifted with the increasing weight of the water. It tilted to the starboard side, inching a little down while the tail settled on the mucky bottom of Long Lake. The great moose that had been wading into the water had fled at the noise of the plane stripping off the tops of the pines. It had run with its peculiar duck-footed gait into the first ring of forest beyond the pond, and it had made an arc, keeping the pond in view, its heart beating heavily in its chest at the approach of a sound coming through the trees.

In the third set of seats behind the pilot, Jill Heatherton could not get Jenky to answer her. Her sister looked *weird*, Jill thought. Really weird. They had been holding hands when the plane started down, but something had changed, something had *departed*, she thought, which made no sense at all.

"Jenky," she said over and over, "wake up."

The plane bulged in next to Jenky. It looked almost like a small explosion, like the time her uncle Azelea had shot a blue jay off a branch in Tennessee. One second the bird had been there, the next it was gone, and she had had the same feeling then as she had now.

Jenky was gone.

"Jenky," she said, reaching over to take her sister's hand again, "come on now."

Someone was yelling, "Open the door, open the door," and someone nearby was moaning. Jill tried to slow her breathing — she could always manage her breathing; it was one of the first things they taught you in ballet class — but now she found she couldn't. She fumbled at her seat belt, trying to get it to release, and she had just clicked it off when the plane shifted again, sliding to the right and scooping down into the lake, or ocean, or whatever body of water it was that came crawling in looking for them all.

No one on earth could have been more surprised at Seldon Eggerts's first thought when the plane stopped than Seldon Eggerts himself.

He thought of Buford.

That stupid, stupid dog. The dog that had been the bane of his existence, his responsibility on trips like these, his cross to bear when he had to get the idiotic animal to sit still for the camera and to play off Web Simon, the obnoxious little redheaded twit who starred in the show. Who else was going to walk the dog on road trips, make sure it was fed and watered? Not the kids, that was for sure. Not any of the network people who loved the dog in the abstract, thought it was the key to the show, but never lifted a finger to feed or walk or clean up – oh, yes, that was part of the care of a dog – and left everything to him.

He stood. He had to tilt sideways and put his hand out on the baggage rack. He saw Walter Eliot yelling something about an open door, or *to open* a door, Seldon couldn't be sure, but he wished the guy would get a grip anyway.

"Hey," Seldon yelled, "where's the pilot?"

"No," someone yelled back, but whether the answer had anything to do with the pilot, Seldon couldn't say.

Seldon turned and pulled open the cargo door. Water sizzled around his feet as the door came open, and he half closed the door to keep the water out. But it was too late. The water ran down toward the nose of the plane, and Seldon felt it ooze into his socks and loafers. The loafers were expensive, darn expensive, and he tried to keep his feet up and away from the water, but it was no use.

The plane shifted again. He lurched to the left and caught himself as he heard Buford from inside the cargo hold, scratching at something.

"Yes," Seldon said to the dog, "I'm coming."

He could barely see the dog crate. It was upside down. The glow of the emergency lights caught Buford's eyes. Seldon had half a notion to let the dog stay, but he didn't like thinking of the conversation he would have to have with Tommy Stevens, the head of programming, if he let the dog go down with the ship.

He leaned half his body into the cargo hold and jiggled the latch to the door. It took him a minute – the crate door was wedged against the side of the plane – but finally the latch popped and the door shot open. Buford fell out like a long hot dog, dripping through the opening buttfirst, then finally plunking into the deepening water. The dog faced the wrong way around.

"Open the door," someone still yelled from the center of the plane. "Open the door."

"Come on," Seldon whispered to Buford. "This way."

The dog – with his long, droopy face – turned around with difficulty in the narrow confines of the cargo hold.

And Seldon, not even sure why he did it, reached out and ran his fingers down the dog's long ears, his eyes growing wet at the sight of the dog's apparent health. *Stupid dog*, he thought. *Stupid, stupid dog.*

Titus pushed open the port-side emergency door. It did not want to open. He had to stand on the arm of a seat and extend his entire body straight up, straining against the weight of the door and the added push of gravity, but at last the door swung back. It made a huge *boom* as it fell against the side of the plane and he heard someone inside scream, but there was no way to make the door open more softly. He kept his hands above his head in case anything fell through the door, but instead he saw nothing but the moon.

It was three-quarters full – waxing or waning, he couldn't remember – and ironically, it sat directly over the open door, as if he had centered its location in a camera's viewfinder. Dead center. The last light of the day entered through the opening, too, and he gradually lowered his arms now that he felt fairly certain nothing else planned to fall off the plane in the next second or two. He tried to boost himself up so he could see out, but the opening was too high. He couldn't pull himself up and scramble through, so he ducked his head back toward the interior of the plane and spoke to Web Simon.

The kid stared at him and didn't move.

"Web," Titus said, "I need a boost."

"I can't," Web said.

"Yes, you can."

Web shook his head.

"If you boost me, I can climb out and then pull you up. We can all get out. It's the only way to exit. The plane is resting on its side, and this is the high point. Come on, don't freeze up on me."

Web shook his head and looked away.

Titus reached over the seat in front of him and tapped E on the shoulder.

"I need a boost," he said when she looked around.

She hadn't moved, he realized. She hadn't done anything except stare straight ahead. *Shock*, he reminded himself. Shock was the first thing you had to think about in an accident. But when he looked again, he realized she still had headphones on and was watching a movie on her iPad.

Watching a movie! The idea, the absurdity of the idea, didn't calculate for him. Who watched a movie while a plane crashed?

"I need a boost!" Titus yelled, frustrated that people were not comprehending the situation. "We can get out this way."

To his surprise, Paul Eliot, the smallest guy in the group, the show's "nerd," slowly climbed over a seat and offered to boost him.

Titus and Paul weren't particularly close. Web and Paul spent the most time together, always talking about made-up stuff that didn't interest Titus. Paul didn't strike Titus as the sort to step forward and assert himself. Now, though, with Paul volunteering to help out, Titus reassessed the kid standing in front of him. Paul was short, true, but he was nimble and clever about everything. Paul almost always had an angle on things, a way to approach a problem. So when he thought about it a second longer, Titus realized it probably made sense that

Paul would rally and offer to help. Paul "got it." He had evaluated the situation as fast as anyone and now stood ready to help.

"Just brace yourself and I'll climb on your back," Titus said. "I can put most of my weight on my arms."

"Go ahead," Paul said.

Titus hoisted himself up, using his feet to climb Paul's back. When he cleared the opening, he swung his rear end down so he could sit and see where they had crashed.

"We're close to shore," he yelled down. "We're on the shore, really."

He put his head back up and looked around. Mountains, water, trees. That was all he saw.

CHAPTER 3

Paul Eliot climbed onto the plane's fuselage beside Titus. It wasn't that hard to do, Paul realized. He was not the most athletic guy in the world, so if he could do it, so could others. The skin of the fuselage, however, was slick and wet. He sat carefully, his legs still back in the body of the plane. Down below, everything felt crazy and disordered. Up here, however, the night was calm. His hands out at his sides to brace himself, he looked around slowly, sensitive to the plane's annoying habit of shifting. Titus sat across from him, his legs also in the door frame. They looked like two prairie dogs, Paul thought, sitting beside their hole.

"We have to get to shore," Titus said.

"How?" Paul asked. He didn't see a way. Or rather, he didn't see an *easy* way. The doorway where they sat rose at least seven or eight feet above the water. To get to shore, you would have to jump or slide off the body of the plane into the water, then swim to land. On a bright, sunny day, it might have been almost fun to try it, but right now, with the sun going down, the moonlight painting the tops of the pines, it didn't seem like a good idea. *Never jump into water you don't know*, Paul thought. That had always been a family rule. Anything could be right under the surface – rocks, a piece of metal from the plane, anything. If you got impaled by a piece of metal up here – wherever "here" was – you were a goner.

"We need to find a rope or something . . . or tie some life jackets together," Titus said, his eyes studying the problem. "I don't know what we should do exactly, but we can't stay in the plane. It could go under."

"This is crazy," Paul said, looking around.

It was getting dark, but he saw the place in outline. They were on a shoreline of a lake, at least he thought it was a lake, and there were a couple million pine trees in every direction. And it was cold. He felt the frigid air spilling down on them, or maybe rising from the water, he couldn't tell. Either way, it was not a night for a swim.

"We have to get people working together," Titus said. "We have to calm down. Can you get your dad to stop yelling?"

Paul nodded. Then, gradually, he realized Titus meant right now. Right this second. He nodded again and held out his hand. Titus grabbed it and lowered Paul back into the plane's interior.

"Dad," Paul said.

His father kept yelling to *open the door. The door* is *open*, Paul wanted to say, but he saw that his father had gone a little nutty. It was weird to see his father like that. It was weird to be calmer than your own father. He reached across the back of a seat and grabbed his dad's hand. His dad shook it off and then slowly, heartbeat by heartbeat, came back to himself. Paul saw his father's personality crawl back behind his eyes again.

"It's open," Paul said. "The door is open."

"Hey. Hey. Heyyyyyyyyyy," Titus yelled.

The interior of the plane gradually went silent. Titus

looked slowly around, trying to assess the situation. That was always the Boy Scout way: *Think, then act.* Too many people did the opposite in an emergency. If you stopped to think, really think, then you could usually sort things out. Leadership was the single most important lesson you learned as an Eagle Scout, and leadership meant keeping your cool and channeling your emotions into productive behavior. That was basic Boy Scout training. Titus said a little thank you to all the Scoutmasters who had trained him up through Scout, Tenderfoot, Second Class, First Class, Star, Life, and now Eagle. He realized he wouldn't trade all that training, all that practice, for a million dollars. People could think scouting was dorky, but he couldn't imagine any better motto than *Be Prepared* for the current situation.

"We need to get off the plane," Titus shouted, then realized his voice was too loud and would only add to the potential panic. He lowered it. "This door opens to the top of the plane. We have to make a rope that we can tie off down here and use to go down the side of the plane. Look around you and find anything that can be tied together. Then pass it to Paul. If you are injured, let us know. If someone near you is injured, then we'll help."

"Jenky won't wake up," Jill Heatherton said. "She looks strange."

Titus caught Mr. Eliot's eye.

"Mr. Eliot," he said, thinking it was best to give Mr. Eliot something to do to keep him from going nutty again, "will you please check on Jenky? The rest of you, start finding things to build a rope. We can make a camp on the shore for tonight. We can get a fire started. But first we need to get out of the plane."

No one said anything. No one moved, either.

"I think the pilot is dead," Suryadi said.

Suryadi's seat was closest to the cockpit, Titus knew.

"We'll check on him," Titus said. "Now, rope, every-one. We need to climb down."

Titus watched as E stood up and pulled two blankets together. She knotted them quickly, then passed them over to Paul. Titus had never seen E act so practically, and it made him wonder what else she could do in a pinch. She was tall and beautiful, and her singing video had gone viral, so he had automatically assumed she wouldn't be much help in the current situation. He assumed she was a diva, a girl super into herself and her looks. But he had been wrong about Paul, and he was wrong about E, apparently. He scolded himself not to judge people hastily, or to jump to conclusions from their outward appearances. He knew better. E might be cute and dance across the computer screens of a couple million viewers, but she also looked calm and completely in control inside the plane's fuselage. He promised himself he wouldn't make such a mistake again.

"Like that, the way E is doing it," Titus said and then got Paul to boost him up again. The stars blinked in the sky and the moon sent a yellow path across the water behind them.

Web tested the blanket rope and felt as though he had lived this particular nightmare before. It took him a second – with people calling below him and Super Scout Titus Summers waiting in the water to help him get his feet under him – to remember what it was. Then it came to him, and he nodded a little in satisfaction at recalling the precise origin of his thought: gym class. It was the day they'd climbed a rope for a grade. It had something to do with the Governor's Physical Fitness Test, and so they had all hung around the bottom of a thick rope, the high end tied to a beam in the ceiling, and were told to climb. Even the girls had to climb, but none of them did. They just pretended and swung from side to side, but the boys had to act macho and climb as high as they could, and Web knew his fat butt and chubby arms were not going to go up a rope any time soon. He grabbed the rope and made some faces and pretended to climb, pantomiming, and everyone had laughed, because he could be funny, he knew, but his feet didn't leave the gym floor.

And here he was again. Back in gym class.

"Just slowly come down," Titus coached. "It isn't that far. If you hold on, I'll be able to grab your feet and lower you. No worries."

"Thanks," Web said, then mumbled, "Super Scout," under his breath.

He lay on his belly and slowly began lowering himself. The surface of the plane's body was slick as butter, and he felt himself slipping. The rope shot through his hands, and he felt himself falling, falling, and then he hit the water. It was cold as anything, freezing in fact, and he shot back up, his breath contracting in his lungs.

"You had to hold on," Titus said.

He had a bloody nose, Web saw.

"Your foot hit my nose!" Titus said, touching his right nostril. "You had to hold on!"

Web felt a grin move across his lips. He had bloodied the great Titus Summers's nose. That was one for the books.

"Sorry," he said to Titus.

"Go that way. You can walk. It's not that deep."

Web put his feet down on the bottom. It was rocky, not muddy like the ponds in western Pennsylvania. Ahead of him, he saw the group assembled, all of them staring at the plane as if they expected it to rise out of the water and take off. Mosquitoes started buzzing in his ears.

Seldon handed Buford up to Paul. It had taken forever to strap Buford into a tiny life jacket. The life jacket formed a harness, and he had tied the makeshift rope into the back of it. They would have to lower the dog, let him slide along the fuselage like a tea bag dropping into hot water. Something like that.

"Got him," Paul said.

"Are you sure?"

"He's not liking this."

"Just lower him quickly. Don't give him a chance to see what's going on."

Seldon heard Buford growl, and he didn't blame him. Then he sounded really angry. The growl turned into a snarl, and Seldon climbed up to the opening and stuck his head out.

"What's happening?" he asked.

But Paul – little, mousy Paul, Seldon marveled – stood on the fuselage, looking over the edge until he heard Titus yell below.

"Got him," Titus said.

Seldon heard people calling Buford from shore. He wondered if the stupid dog could swim. All animals could swim naturally, he remembered, except humans. But Buford was just stupid enough to swim the wrong way.

Before he could say or do anything else, the plane shifted again. It was the water seeping on board, Seldon guessed. It was everywhere now, as high as the seat backs in places, and it was probably pushing air out of some cavities, weighting others with its density. Eventually, Seldon thought, the plane would settle once and for all on its belly.

"You're next," Paul said from the open door above him, his head sticking through like an upside-down Spider-Man.

"What about..." Seldon said, moving his chin to indicate Jenky and the pilot.

"We'll get them in the morning," Paul said. "Right now we have to get away from the plane. It feels like it's going to go under."

"Seems weird to leave them...."

"In the morning," Paul said. "Safety first."

It made sense, Seldon agreed. But it was a hard kind of sense. He climbed into position, then used the bags they had placed as steps to scramble through the door opening. Paul showed him how to roll on his belly and hold on to the rope as it went over the edge. Seldon lowered himself carefully until he felt Titus grab his feet. Twice more hand-over-hand, and his feet plunged into the water.

My loafers, he thought.

Then he turned to see Buford paddling in circles. The dog wore his ridiculous life jacket and seemed to be waiting for him. Seldon reluctantly followed him to shore.

E knew what they needed to do from camping trips with her parents, but she couldn't get anyone's attention. Everyone talked at once. That was understandable, given what had happened, but it didn't help. Talk seldom helped, she thought. She heard the voices going round and round, recounting what they had experienced during the crash, all the "likes" and "you knows," all the stories trying to explain what had happened when it was clear no one knew what had happened. What was the point, she wondered?

The facts were simple: They were a bunch of kids from a semilame television show who'd had the bad fortune to crash in what looked like a complete wilderness. They had no adults along except for Seldon Eggerts, the show's producer, and Walter Eliot, Paul's father, who was the sort of nerdy middle-aged man who thought it gained him props when he told people he had an authentic Lionel Train set in the basement. Mr. Eliot didn't really belong on the plane, but he had wheedled his way on board, claiming he was Paul's manager or something. No one believed it, least of all Paul, but sometimes you had to pretend what people wanted you to pretend. Now they were all blabbing, probably half in shock, but it was getting colder, and no one seemed bothered by that fact.

When she couldn't stand it anymore, she made a high-pitched screeching sound. It was from a cartoon – she had forgotten which one – and was a tactic that she and her brother used in the backseat of the family car on long trips when her parents hopped out to get gas or use the restroom. It drove the other person insane. The trick was to start low, just on the outside of people's hearing range, then incrementally increase the volume until it became annoyingly painful. Then go a little further. Her brother, Ralphy, called it the Hippo Hurricane. It wasn't a bad name.

So she used the Hippo Hurricane until gradually, one by one, people turned to face her. When she had all of their attention, she lowered the volume and partially swallowed the sound. She didn't want them to think they could get her to click it off just like that.

"We need a fire," she said. "Big duh, I know, but we need it now. We can talk later."

No one moved.

"Now," she said, underlining the word with intonation, "everyone collect wood if you're not injured. There's plenty here on the beach. We'll build a fire right here."

"What was that sound?" someone asked, but at least people began moving.

"She's right," someone else said, but it was too dark to see who had said it.

E walked down the shoreline, aware of other people moving around, too. They needed a fire pronto. Whatever else happened, a fire was a top priority, because it was cold and everyone was wet. She couldn't say for sure, but she imagined the temperature had fallen into the forties. At least. She could see her breath sometimes when she bent to pick up hunks of pine, and the rocks under her feet were slippery with frost.

When she had a good bundle, she stopped and looked around. She deliberately forced herself to take inventory. They were on the shoreline of a lake. The lake went on forever. Beyond the lake, she spotted the dim outline of mountains. She knew the sun set in the west. So the lakeside camp looked westward, because the sun set behind the mountains and threw its last light across the lake. That was worth knowing, she figured. Her dad had always made her take notice of things like that. He had always said there was a difference between look-ing and observing, which was something he'd gotten out of Sherlock Holmes. But she knew what he meant. It was important to *see*, not just let your eyes bounce off things with a kind of wild monkey vision.

She carried an armload of wood back to the group and dropped it in the pile she had put together.

"Everyone should get more wood," she announced to people as they streamed in and out. "You always need more than you think you do."

"Who has a match?" Web asked, ignoring her. "And no one's found a knife? If I had a knife, I could whittle some shavings and it would be a lot easier to start a fire."

He bent over the ring where they hoped to build a fire. He was probably the last person who should be trying to make a fire, E thought, but she didn't think it would help to point it out.

"Come on," she said to Jill. "Help me."

Jill walked behind her like a robot. E didn't blame her. Jenky was still on the plane.

"I'll load you up," E said to Jill when they found another bunch of driftwood. "Just hold out your arms."

Jill did as she was told. E slapped at the mosquitoes around her own head. The bugs were intense. Beyond intense. Every time you breathed, you sucked in insects. Stick by stick, she loaded Jill's arms. E felt like the mad scientist with the evil assistant, Igor. Jill just looked dead in the eyes.

"Do you have lip gloss or Vaseline?" Titus asked when they came back.

"Why?" E asked.

"Oil-based. You can make a wicked fire-starter with Vaseline," he answered.

E tapped her pockets. Her clothes were soaked. She found a tiny tub of lip gloss in her jeans pocket.

"Here," she said.

Titus handed it to Web. Web smooched some paper

around in the lip gloss, then put it under the bunch of twigs he had gathered. Titus squatted next to him and added pine needles. That made more sense, E knew. She had made enough beach fires with her parents. They always used pine needles and pinecones.

"Go ahead," Titus said.

The fire started like a tiny old man dancing in an empty room. Then, slowly, it began to grow. Once, Titus loaded on too much pine, and E worried that he had put it out, but then the flame began to lick around it. She grew conscious of everyone circling the tiny flame, rooting for it to grow. Web kept blowing on the bottom, which wasn't always a bad idea, but it could also kill the flames. Fortunately, the wood was so dry and seasoned that it began snapping and throwing sparks almost immediately. E felt a trickle of pride that the fire had been her idea. It threw light when it grew to knee height, and she saw people's outlines slowly emerge from the darkness: the survivors, the ones who had come flying in like an arrow from the sky.

CHAPTER 4

Suryadi looked at his hand. He had just finished reaching under his shirt to touch his side at the warm place. That's what he called the center of the pain. He did not want to think about what it might be. Once, in his native village near Kuta Puri, he had seen a fisherman come in after being attacked by a shark. The man had been spearfishing, and the frenzied movement of the speared fish, the bloody bodies attached to a stringer at the fisherman's belt, had attracted the shark. The man had been bitten in the side and under the right arm, and now Suryadi thought of his own side as though it had been bitten by a shark. That was impossible, of course, but something had wounded him in the ribs, and now he had a warm place that throbbed and quivered and felt empty. Yes, empty. Blood tried to fill the empty warm place.

It had been brutally painful to climb down the rope from the plane and to walk through the icy water, but now the pain had turned into something violent and stiff. His hand, when he moved it subtly toward the fire, displayed lines of blood. He knew he should tell someone that he had sustained an injury, but he felt reluctant. He did not know these people – he had only met them a week ago, when he was flown to America for a casting session. He was an outsider here, a feeling he was not used to at home, and it did no good to pretend otherwise. He supposed he should speak to Mr. Eggerts, who wanted them to call him Seldon, but Mr. Eggerts seemed preoccupied by the dog, Buford. No, it was better to wait and see how things would go. When he saw how things arranged themselves, then he could decide what to do about the warm place.

He moved closer to the fire. He listened to Seldon talk about rescue. The man's mouth moved, but Suryadi had difficulty taking in the words. Because he was the show's producer, Seldon knew the timetable, when they were expected in Alaska, who would be aware of the plane's disappearance. Suryadi tried to listen, tried to follow Seldon's reasoning, but he felt himself fading in and out of consciousness. Cold pressed against his back. The entire forest, as far as he could see, pressed against his back. The fire could not give him enough heat. He shivered. His body needed something he couldn't give it.

". . . I'm sure the pilot filed a flight plan. That's the law," Seldon said from his position across the fire. "And when they see we haven't arrived, they're going to come looking."

"Seldon's right," Mr. Eliot said. "As horrible as our situation is right now, we have to stay optimistic. There's no reason not to think they are on their way. Or will be first thing in the morning, anyway."

"We should have a signal fire ready," Titus said. "There's plenty of wood. We have that going for us."

Suryadi nodded, though he wasn't sure what he was nodding for. The warm place felt bigger, wider beneath his shirt. The dog had already been over twice to sniff at him. Suryadi wondered if blood didn't attract bears. If blood attracted sharks under the water, why not bears in country like this? It was possible. If the dog could smell it, then a bear could smell it.

"We need to keep collecting wood," E said when the two older men stopped talking about rescue and flight plans. "That's what we should be doing."

Suryadi looked at the girl called E. She was very pretty. He had seen her on YouTube, in a singing video, before he had met her. She was the first person he had ever met who was somewhat famous. She would be a star someday, he imagined. Maybe she already was.

"We need to stay in teams. A buddy system," Titus said. "And everyone should stay where they can see the fire."

"There are blankets on the plane," Web said. "Maybe we should get some blankets."

"I don't think we should go on the plane again until we can see what's what," Paul Eliot said. "That's my opinion. Maybe in the morning we can go on."

"In the morning," his dad agreed.

And that's when Suryadi felt the warm place pull something away from his center of gravity. From his balance. He squatted down, his eyes on the flames, and he wanted to say something, something about the shark and the fisherman, the eyes of the fisherman as the man had rested on the canoe, his ribs white and brilliant in the harsh sunlight, the glistening water winking and playing and pretending to be innocent behind him. He remembered the man's eyes, the expression the man had that said everything he needed to know about his injury, or about sharks jamming their teeth deeper into his side.

That was the last thing Suryadi thought before he tilted sideways and fell, his head missing the outer ring of the fire by inches.

"It's so dark," Web said, his arms half-filled with sticks of wood. "We are sitting ducks if any zombies attack."

"Shut up," Paul said, his body bent over a bunch of white driftwood. The driftwood, Web reflected, looked like bones.

"I'm just saying," Web said, surprised that Paul didn't want to play along. They had talked a lot about zombies and about comics in general. It was an old conversational thread between them. "We've got nothing. Not one zombie weapon."

"I'm more worried about bears," Paul said. "And the cold. The cold can kill us. It's not pretend."

"Still," Web said, not sure where he wanted to go with the conversation.

It *was* cold. Way cold. He had no socks on, no overcoat, no sweater. It had been hot in LA, almost ninety, when they had taken off, and Web had worn his usual polo shirt, baggy shorts, and orange Crocs. Wardrobe would make him wear whatever it wanted him to wear once they got to the shoot, so it made no sense to worry about clothes for the plane ride. So now he was dressed for a Los Angeles August afternoon, for the sweet couch in front of his basement game station, to be honest, but he had been rerouted to the tundra. It was worse than zombies.

"It's freezing," Web said. "Let's get back to the fire."

"We need as much as we can carry."

"I've got my load."

"But I haven't. And we're on the buddy system."

"The fire is right over there," Web said. "Titus is being a little heavy-handed, don't you think? We're not babies."

Paul didn't answer. He finally had his arms full of brittle-looking wood.

"Okay," he said.

"You think they'll come looking for us?" Web asked, his arms aching with the weight of the wood.

"Of course they will."

"What if they don't?"

Paul began walking back to the fire.

"We're in serious trouble if they don't," Paul said.

"That's what I'm saying. Did you see that kid Suryadi keel over?"

Paul nodded. At least Web thought he nodded. It was hard to see in the dark. It was hard to even walk in the dark, because Web nearly stumbled twice on the uneven river stones. It was like walking on marbles.

"He's paired up with Jill," Paul said. "They're staying by the fire."

"I know that," Web said, feeling his arms begging to drop the wood. "She's completely zapped."

"Shhhh." Paul shushed him.

Web stumbled the last few steps and chucked his wood on the pile beside the fire. His hands felt frozen, and his legs burned from the aftermath of so many mosquito bites. He inched over to the fire. People had dragged over larger rocks or pieces of logs for seats. He plunked down on a gnarly pine stump and leaned as close as he could to the flames. The fire was decent. It was nearly too hot on your front, but your back was in the Arctic.

He looked over at Suryadi. The kid lay on the ground, his eyes straight up at the stars.

"Where's your buddy?" he asked the kid, but his voice was drowned out by Seldon dropping an armful of wood onto the pile. Still, they were supposed to stay together, even the two lame-os at the fire. If he had to stick with a buddy, then he expected everyone else to stick with a buddy.

"Where's Jill?" he asked, and the kid lifted his hand and pointed toward the forest behind them.

Δ   Δ   Δ

Jill walked like Frankenstein's monster, her hands out in front of her, her eyes searching for the light of the fire. But it was dark. It was all much darker than she could have believed, and now the forest seemed to stretch in every direction without any borders or definition. If you had told her ten minutes before that she could get lost by slipping into the woods to go to the bathroom, she would have said that was crazy.

I'm just going over there, she had told her so-called buddy, Suryadi. She didn't tell him why she had to go over there and she didn't particularly care if he figured it out. She was buddies with Suryadi, the Indonesian boy with the bloody shirt, and she wasn't about to ask him to accompany her into the bushes even if he was able. What she really wanted, what she felt down in her belly, was the twin need for her sister. She wanted Jenky, her other half, her best friend, but that, she knew, wasn't going to happen.

That isn't going to happen, she told herself again. *Ever.*

That was impossible to think about, to make sense of, to get a handle on. She shut it out as much as she could, and after she finished in the bushes, she looked around, ready to hurry back to the fire, but the fire wasn't there. It wasn't anywhere. She smelled wood smoke, sort of, but even that didn't seem to come from any specific direction. Insects swarmed around her and made finding her way back to the fire even more difficult. She felt – in the darkness, with the mosquitoes churning around her, the incessant buzz in her ears, and the bug taste in each breath – that she might go completely nuts.

Not a little nuts. Not pretend nuts like when you couldn't find your pen at school or the container of yogurt you had hidden in the fridge. She felt on the edge as she had never been on the edge before. And she was uncertain if she could hold it all together.

That's why she walked like Frankenstein's monster. That's why she kept running into everything.

She had never been in woods like these. Or woods even close to these. She and Jenky used to play in a rhododendron patch on the side of the house. That was as close as she had ever come to being in the woods. But now logs ran everywhere, up and down, on the ground and as leaners, and she supposed she should stop and try to figure things out, or call, but she felt the sizzle of adrenaline zipping through her veins.

It was easier to move than to think.

Easier to move than to remember.

Then, far away, she heard someone calling her name. It came faintly through the woods, and at first she didn't want to answer. She didn't want *them*. She wanted Jenky, or her parents, or anyone who would really understand what it meant to be without your twin for the first time. *The first time in your life.* At the same moment, though, the bugs started drilling into her neck, under her hair in the back, and she knew they had found a vulnerable spot. She slapped at them and tried to brush them off her skin, but a thousand insects replaced the ones she shook away.

She called for help.

It was weird, though, because she couldn't remember making the effort to call for help an instant after she had done it. It was as if a voice had come up through her lungs and out of her mouth, but it didn't belong to her. She had not generated it. It simply shot out into the blackness and seemed to go up and up and up as if she had tried to hit a high, operatic note. Laced into the call, she detected elements of panic and terror that she didn't feel consciously, but they were undeniable. It was the call of someone drowning or falling, and it came again, shooting up through her mouth and throat, and she slumped down onto the wet logs when she finished and listened to people shouting back and forth.

Over here, someone yelled, a boy.

Over this way. Jill? Jill, where are you?

It's too dark! someone shouted.

Then suddenly someone with a light stood in front of her. It was nearly like magic.

"Got her!" someone yelled.

It was a boy. It was Titus.

"You should have a buddy," he said.

"He's injured."

"Well, still."

Then a few others crashed up through the woods next to Titus. Two had flashlights. The light was painful to look at.

"Just follow us out," someone – not Titus, but she couldn't see who spoke – said. It was a girl.

Jill nodded. She followed them again like Frankenstein's monster, her hands up to protect her eyes from the twigs and branches that tried to impale her.

Then, before she knew what had happened, someone had her beside the fire again, and the flames jumped up and made the sky orange, but only for a second, only spark by spark.

It was late, sometime well after midnight, when Walter Eliot tapped Seldon Eggerts on the shoulder and whispered in his ear.

"Can I talk to you?" Walter Eliot asked.

Walter watched Seldon Eggerts shake himself. Seldon had been half-asleep beside the fire. The basset hound had curled beside him. They both looked up, half-awake, fully annoyed.

"What is it?" Seldon asked.

"I need to talk to you," Walter said. "Over there."

"Over where?" Seldon asked, sitting up slowly and looking around him.

"Away from the fire," Walter said. "You know, adult to adult."

Seldon sighed and slowly pushed himself to his feet. The dog uncurled and shook itself. Walter led them away. He saw Seldon nearly fall, then catch himself. The dog trotted easily beside him.

"What is it?" Seldon asked when they had gone about twenty yards from the fire. "It's freezing."

"A little farther," Walter said. "Sound carries over water."

Maybe it was getting lighter, Walter thought. He certainly hoped so. His body ached and his nerves felt on edge. But he needed to go over things with Eggerts. That much was clear.

"Okay," Walter said when they reached a sufficient distance.

"What's this all about?" Seldon asked, his voice betraying his annoyance. "Why did you wake me up?"

"I figured we needed a chance to talk away from the kids," Walter said, his voice low and straight between them. "About our circumstances."

"What about our circumstances?"

"I just figured tomorrow . . . well, we should have a unified front. We should have a clear plan."

"There isn't a clear plan. That's the nature of these things."

"I mean about rescue. About our chances."

"Are you asking if I think someone is looking for us? I don't know. No one knows. I would imagine they are, but you never know. In case you didn't notice, this was a small plane. It's not part of any airline. It's a guide service, really."

"So you don't know if the pilot filed a flight plan?"

"I assume he did, but I don't know for certain. Why are we talking about this in the middle of the night? We can't do anything about it right now."

"I thought we might be able to be more frank without the kids listening in."

Walter watched Seldon reach down and pet the dog. That was that thing, he realized. That was that thing that other people did around him. People often appeared annoyed somehow with him, and they did things like that: stapled papers or pet dogs or put files together. Walter had never been certain why he brought out that behavior in others, but he knew he did. In everyone but his son. His son never betrayed his lack of interest that way.

"Listen, Walter," Seldon said, standing up from petting the dog finally, "if you think I'm in charge of this mission, then you need to think again. I have no idea what to do. I don't think anyone does. As far as what's behind us, or ahead of us, for that matter, I have no idea. The pilot came highly recommended, so I imagine he did file a flight plan. And I also imagine he put out an SOS, but I can't say for certain if he did. Maybe the plane has a beacon on it. I don't know. I have no idea where we are. We were going north from Anchorage. That's about as good as I can do."

"Near the Brooks Range," Walter said, mostly to reassure himself.

"If you say so. In the morning, we may have a better idea. It's possible the radio works on the plane, but I doubt it. Even if it did work, I'd be the last one to get it operating. I have no desire to be Cub Scout leader here. Frankly, Titus knows much more about this type of thing than I do. He's an Eagle Scout, at least. I can't speak for you, but I bet he knows more than you, too. So why don't we go back to sleep?"

"I thought it best to have a plan when they wake up."

Seldon bent and petted the dog again.

"We're in trouble," Seldon said. "We'll try our best to fix things. That's the whole plan, as far as I can see."

"I just thought as adults . . ."

"These kids aren't stupid, Walter. They know the situation as well as we do. If someone doesn't come to get us out of here, we're dead meat."

"You really think so?"

Seldon nodded. Then he turned around and went back to the fire.

CHAPTER 5

Fuel was not a problem, Titus realized. *Gathering* fuel might be. Getting people to see the need to plan ahead definitely would be, but fuel was plentiful. Wherever the lake was situated on a map, deep forest surrounded it. Mounds and jumbles of wood cluttered the shoreline and to gather it simply required time and energy. Titus imagined the wood had been lifted onto the shore by the ice during the winter. When you sighted along it carefully from the side, you saw that it probably represented the high-tide line.

Or high ice line. Or snow line. Or whatever.

But that also meant you needed to build your structures farther away from the water than the line.

That's what went through his head.

The other thing that went through his head was the sunrise.

It came from behind them. At first, it appeared as if the dark had simply slipped away like a sheet pulled back to reveal old, dusty furniture. He tipped forward on his knees and put more wood into the fire. It was a good fire now, hot and filled with coals, and he had to look away to gauge the sun's slowly building strength. He saw the beach, the rocky shore, for what it was: nothing more than a thumbnail, a point of land that stuck out into the lake's body. The light revealed no new landmarks, nothing to give a framework for where they had landed. Yes, he saw mountains off to the north, and he saw more trees than he had ever seen in his life, but nothing showed any sign of human habitation. No smoke trails, no church steeples, no bridge spans. Nothing but trees and water and sky.

He stood and walked to the water's edge. He squatted next to it and washed his face and hands. That was a survival technique, he remembered. Keep things orderly, keep to routines, establish rules even when there were no rules. Wash your face, brush your teeth, comb your hair. To do otherwise was to give in to the animal side of things, the impulse you felt to go running blindly through the woods like a startled deer. Or like a startled Jill. She didn't know how lucky they had been to find her. She didn't realize how easy it was to let the forest swallow you. Even though it had felt like no big deal in the end, Titus knew they had avoided a bad situation. He knew he had to keep an eye on her. She was not in a good place mentally.

"You're awake?" Walter Eliot said.

He did not come from the fire, Titus noted. He came from down the shoreline.

"I guess I am," Titus answered.

"I couldn't sleep," Walter Eliot said. "I did a little scouting instead."

"We should probably stay together, Mr. Eliot. If you got lost or hurt yourself, we wouldn't know where to look for you. Jill was lost last night for a few minutes, and it could have easily gone another way. We were lucky we noticed she was gone so quickly. Another fifteen minutes and she might have been too far into the woods to find."

"I didn't go far. I thought maybe I could make sense of where we landed, but it's just a big lake in the middle of nowhere."

Titus nodded and stood. He remembered Mr. Eliot asking over and over again for someone to open the door.

"What do you think our first plan should be?" Mr. Eliot asked.

Titus looked at the older man. Something didn't seem quite right with Mr. Eliot, but Titus couldn't point to anything in particular. Maybe it was a form of panic or worry, but the man seemed impatient, as if everything should have an answer right away. Titus looked out over the water so he wouldn't have to meet Mr. Eliot's eyes.

"We have a lot of work we can do," Titus said, giving voice to things he had already thought about through the night. "We should keep everyone busy, that's the first thing. We need to build structures. Shelters, because it could rain anytime. It already rained a little during the night. We probably need to establish a latrine so our waste doesn't contaminate the water. Collect wood, a lot of wood. We have to think about food, too. There's probably some on the plane, but it won't last forever."

"Forever!" Mr. Eliot said, his voice almost like a bark of surprise. "There will be a full-out search for us! I'm sure they're in the air right now."

"Probably so. I hope so. But meanwhile we're here. We need to salvage whatever we can from the plane. We might be able to use some of the plane parts for building materials . . . for roofs and things. We should probably divide up into teams and give every team a job. We can rotate the jobs eventually, but for the time being we need to make careful steps. We need to stay organized. We almost lost Jill because we weren't organized."

Titus heard people moving beside the fire. Light continued to build behind them. He wondered if it was a good thing to be positioned so the sun didn't hit you immediately in the morning, or if they would be better off moving across the lake. It was amazing, he reflected, how much had to be done to make them even marginally safe and comfortable. It was like a lot of the camping he had done, multiplied many times over.

"What about the pilot and the girl?"

"We'll take a team in and bring them out. And we'll give them a respectable burial away from here. I'm worried about Jill, but we can only do so much. The big thing is to stay active. All of us. Even if we make poor decisions sometimes, it's better to be active."

"These bugs..." Mr. Eliot said and slapped at the mosquitoes that had lifted around them.

"We need a smudge fire to keep them down. The good news is we should have a frost pretty soon. That will kill them off."

"You don't really think we'll be here until the frost, do you?"

"Don't think, just plan," Titus said.

That was something he had learned in Scouts.

He left Mr. Eliot at the water's edge and walked back to the fire.

Paul Eliot climbed the rope ladder into the plane's fuselage for what had to be the thirtieth time. It reminded him of a nature documentary he had once seen on leafcutter ants of Central America. Leafcutter ants laid down a chemical trail, and then all the ants in a colony trudged along it, all of them carrying something. They brought in leaves, primarily, to form a food store. At least that's what Paul remembered. He remembered being mesmerized by the ants, and he had even lobbied for an ant farm for Christmas. His dad had pointed out the risk of ant farms, how they could tip over and release the ants, and no one wanted that.

But Paul did. He wanted that.

Not that he wanted it to tip over. He had simply wanted an ant colony, but his dad had vetoed it.

Anyway, that was a different time, a different place. A *way* different place. Thinking about an ant farm had to be on a top-ten list of strange things to think about while on an improvised ladder climbing into the dead fuselage of a plane beside a lake in the shadow of the Brooks Range. That's what Paul thought about, how each one of them was like an ant with a job to do to support the colony.

He also thought how much his hands and legs and back hurt.

But they were making progress. And when he stuck his head up to the height of the doorway on the upside of the plane, E met him. She wore a bandanna over her head, and she looked cool. It was typical of E that she could look fashionable even while emptying a plane of its contents.

"Anything else?" Paul asked.

She shook her head. They had been working all morning and into the afternoon.

"I'm going to take a break. We've got everything," she said.

"Everything?" he asked.

She shrugged. Paul was the team captain on the plane team, at least in theory, but everyone listened to E anyway. He knew he did. She was tall and smart and very capable.

"Web is still up in the cockpit working on the radio," she said, starting to climb out. "It's busted up and probably won't work, but what the heck? It's worth a try."

"And it gets him out of doing other work," Paul said, his voice going low. Web had become the running joke of the plane team because he was lazy and a know-it-all.

E smiled. She sat on the edge of the doorway and looked down at the camp. The building team had already pulled out a dozen dead fir trees and piled them in a stack near the fireplace. They had also been digging a wide, shallow hole in the beach.

"It's starting to look like a camp," E said, nodding at the shoreline.

"Lucky we have Titus with us."

"I always thought scouting was pretty lame," E said. "Until now. Now it seems pretty smart."

"He says these are just temporary huts."

"It's a pretty good idea, though. What did he think of the crossbow we found?"

"He loved it. But he said we'd stand a better chance of catching fish than hunting anything."

E nodded. It was kind of cool, Paul thought, that the crash had made it possible for him to talk to E. Made it possible that they could be on the same team, seek the same ends, do the same job. Before the crash, E hadn't really acknowledged him. She had always been polite, he admitted, but hadn't engaged with anyone, so to speak. Now she was. Now she was probably the second in command behind Titus. It turned out she was friendly and strong and funny.

"Is that it?" Seldon called from the water below them.

He stood with his hand up to his eyes for shade, looking up at them.

He was another leafcutter ant on the plane team, Paul thought. The one who went from the plane to the shore, then back again. It went E to Paul, Paul to Seldon, Seldon to shore. Web did nothing except pretend to work on the radio.

"Looks like it. It's everything we can get to without tools," Paul said.

"Did you get all the food?"

"Yep," Paul said.

E nodded.

"Okay," Seldon said, "then I'm going to go up on the beach for a while. I'm getting cold in this water."

"You can go ahead," Paul said to E. "I'll go check on Web."

"He's not getting anywhere."

"Well, he's on the team, so I should check."

He had to trade places with E. She squeezed by him and shimmied down the ladder. Paul went the other way, climbing into the dark interior of the plane. Water had seeped into the plane and filled it up to the seats. It was a sloppy mess, with things floating and swirling in the water. Now and then, the plane groaned or shuddered, and you could feel it going deeper. It couldn't go far, and there was a discussion about turning the plane into their sleeping compartment, but it was too wet and disgusting. They were better off on land.

Paul waded down the aisle to the cockpit.

"Any luck?" he asked Web as he sloshed into the nose area.

"Naw," Web said.

He had his head ducked under the steering apparatus. Paul couldn't say for sure, but it looked like Web had stuck his head under there when he heard Paul approach. That was the kind of thing that Web did. He was sneaky and smart and lazy, and Paul admired some of that, he did, but the kid drove him nuts mostly.

But Web knew the most about electronics. And it was worth letting him fiddle with the radio.

"You would think it would have a rescue beacon or something," Paul said.

"I checked it. This plane is old, you know? Really old."

"How do you know?"

"Some of the manual was in here," Web said, pointing to a small leather box near the pilot's seat. "It's not complete, but some of it's from the seventies."

"The nineteen seventies?" Paul asked.

Web nodded and pulled himself up from the space under the steering apparatus.

"I think it's shot," Web said. "Kaput."

"Can you use anything else?"

"Like what?" Web asked.

"I don't know. Use the battery to give us some light. Anything. Titus said we should all think outside the box."

"Titus doesn't know everything. It's not exactly rocket science to pull some trees out of the woods and dig a ditch."

Paul looked out the cockpit window. Web had a front-row seat to see all the leafcutter ants going back and forth.

"Well, he says any plan is better than no plan."

"That's about the dumbest thing I've ever heard."

"I think he means to keep people positive."

"So, if you're lost it's better to go deeper into the woods than to sit down and figure things out? Is that what Titus recommends?"

"Look," Paul said, "everyone is doing the best he or she can. Titus is trying to help."

Web shrugged. Then he smiled as if he had just hit on an idea.

"You could fight zombies better from up here than down on the ground," he said. "This wouldn't make a bad zombie-fighting headquarters."

Paul nodded. He knew Web had brought up zombies again because that was what they used to talk about and that was the only way Web knew how to be friends. It was kind of pitiful given the circumstances, but Paul didn't have the heart to say so.

"It would be pretty good," Paul said to give Web something neutral to talk about. "It would be easy to defend."

"Wicked easy to defend," Web said, smiling. "And with that crossbow we found? I'm telling you, we could live through a zombie attack in here."

"Okay, well, we're going to call it a day. We've got everything we can get to easily. Tomorrow, we can come back in and dig around some more. We can help on the buildings while there is still light."

"If we could figure out a way to drain the water away, we'd be better off in here."

"That wouldn't be easy the way the plane is situated. It's going to keep sinking and settling."

"We should figure out a way to get it up on the shore. Then we'd have a real shelter."

"Well, maybe."

Paul slapped Web on the shoulder. He wasn't sure why he did it, but he felt sort of sorry for the kid. Web didn't have many friends in the group, and that had to be difficult. Paul watched Web smile and slip out from behind the steering apparatus.

That was the other thing about the crash, Paul realized. Once everything was stripped away, it was really easy to see what people were like.

Suryadi knew the warm place had grown bigger. He felt it in his side, the gap of flesh growing bigger every minute, every hour, every breath. Flies found the warm place without a problem. They knew. They might as well have formed an arrow and pointed at the blood oozing out of his side.

He wanted to concentrate on the warm place, to see if he could send his mind around it to discover its true dimensions, but Jill, his so-called buddy, had come to squat beside him and repeated something. She knew a little about the warm place.

"Something something something . . . move," she said and motioned with her chin toward the lodge they were building behind him.

He shook his head.

He didn't know what she had said.

"Mr. Eliot?" the girl called, standing for a second before she squatted back in front of Suryadi. "We need to do something with him."

Suryadi shook his head. He wasn't sure why he wanted to keep the warm place secret, but he did. He closed his eyes and leaned back. Sometimes, if he gained just the right posture, the pain went away. It was good to have the pain removed, but it was also true that the pain returned even more intensely when it swam back up his bloodstream. He had come to think of the shark, the shark that bit the fisherman back in Indonesia, as the pain that swam through his veins.

He felt more than saw the older man step beside the fire and block the sun. The man did not seem to like being called on to examine the wound.

"What is it?" he asked Jill.

"He's got it all clamped up, and he won't show anyone. He's bleeding."

"A lot?"

"Some. I don't know."

"What's the story?" the man asked, but whether he asked the girl or directed the question to him, Suryadi couldn't say.

The girl bent forward and waved her hand to chase away the flies.

"We need to look at it," she said with a loud voice. She said it as if he, Suryadi, were a child and couldn't understand. She put spaces between each word.

Suryadi pretended not to understand.

"We looked at it once, didn't we?" Mr. Eliot asked. "Back in the plane."

"That was last night. He needs some attention."

"Well, I'm not a doctor."

"No one here is a doctor," Jill said.

Suryadi dozed away and then woke up with a start when the shark bit more deeply into his side. He wasn't sure how long he had passed out, but when he regained consciousness, his shirt was open and the girl had a wet cloth against his side to clean the cut.

"There's something in there," the girl said.

Mr. Eliot watched over her shoulder.

"Like what?"

"I can see the tip of something, but I don't know. Something went into his side."

Suryadi closed his eyes. When he opened his eyes again, three or four people stood around him. They all bent and looked at the warm place. They reminded him of chickens, their heads bobbing up and down. It made him want to laugh or kick at them; he couldn't say which was the more attractive option. He wanted them to leave him alone. He wanted his father to come and get him. It had been his father's idea to get him on the show in the first place. *A good experience*, his father had said. He wondered what his father would say now.

"Let's lift him into the shelter," Titus said.

"Is it ready?" Mr. Eliot asked.

"For the time being, it is."

Then Suryadi felt his body leave the ground. He wasn't entirely certain they carried him. It was conceivable that he floated. His mind, his thoughts, felt like a pale balloon dangling from a string attached to his body. Sometimes the thoughts dropped down and bounced against his body, and other times they floated off and away. Then the sky closed over him. He heard them say, *this way, no, right here, easy, slowly,* and then he understood what they had been building. They had dug a waist-deep hole in the beach, then used pine trees to construct a circular shelter. They had a tarp suspended over the top, but more pine trees, too, and the result was comfortable and dry and less filled with insects than outside. It resembled a *honay*, the traditional hut of Indonesia, and it pleased him to be inside it.

"Thank you," Suryadi said.

The girl, Jill, sank down beside him. She lifted her hand and kept the flies away. She knew about the warm place. They all did now. Suryadi closed his eyes and smelled the pine and wood smoke.

CHAPTER 6

E stopped on her way to the food station and adjusted
a corner tree that had popped loose. When she had
it back in position – she was the tallest of the group
and had been called on to do the top tier – she backed
away, studying her work. It looked solid, she thought.
Titus had been correct: They needed a temporary shelter, and this one would work. It wouldn't last forever, and
it would be useless against colder temperatures, but for
the time being, it served their purpose.

And the design, she admitted, was truly quite clever.

First they had dug a circular area – call it a basement, she thought – about four feet down into the beach.
Then they had pounded poles into the area around the
circle, leaving enough room for benches around the ring.

The poles only went up about six feet, but given the depth of the basement that gave them a ten-foot-high ceiling. Then, under Titus's guidance, they had woven young pine trees into a thatch that created a green, fragrant wall. It was simple, really. Now they had an entire structure built in the middle of the beach, and inside, you could get away from the worst of the insects. Not bad for their first full day's work.

There had been a short, heated debate about whether it was safe to have a fire inside the hut – if the tree boughs dried out and a spark got to them, they would go up like a flare – but Titus had said given the greenness of the trees and the dampness from the rain, it would probably be okay as long as they kept the fire low. Extremely low. Besides, he said, and she agreed, they needed a center to cling to, a place where they could come and have tribal meetings.

So the hut was complete, she realized, circling a little to see the top tier and the blue tarp covering the roof. They had shelter, at least, and a place to get out of the rain. Rain that – by the look of the sky – stood ready to come in over the lake at any minute.

She stared at the sky for a moment, half hoping to see a plane patrolling overhead, then she shrugged and walked to a second blue tarp stretched out on the ground, where Seldon Eggerts and Walter Eliot had assembled everything they had recovered from the plane.

"How's it look?" she asked the group.

There had been a ton of speculation about what was on the plane, but now, as she peeked past Seldon Eggerts's shoulder, she was astonished to see how little had been salvaged. Working on the plane that morning and afternoon, it had seemed like a ton of trips, but now the result was fairly meager. Seldon had put the food to one side, tools to the other, and odds and ends in a third pile. The crossbow – something the pilot had kept in a tiny compartment behind his seat – stood out in its own place. E wasn't interested in it, but she knew the boys had been excited at its discovery. She would have preferred that they'd found a sharp knife.

"Not great," Web said. "We're in trouble."

He knelt on the opposite side of the tarp from Seldon Eggerts and Walter Eliot. It made E shiver a little to see Web now wore some of the pilot's clothing. Web had come on the shoot in his ridiculous shorts and a pair of Crocs, and if it hadn't been for the pilot's clothing, he would have been in a bad way. Still, it made her uneasy. She kept her eyes on Buford. The basset hound sat beside Web, his silly, long body tucked into a sitting position that didn't quite work.

"Keep it positive," Walter Eliot said to Web.

"We are positively in trouble," Web said and grinned, but no one else found him funny.

"It's not great," Seldon said, his eyes down to study the food. "I thought there would be more food. I guess they don't need to provide much food on such a short trip."

E looked closely at the food pile. It was paltry. Mostly, she thought, it looked like a supply for the pilot, a kind of backup picnic lunch he might have packed for himself. He had a box of instant oatmeal, a half sandwich – ham, she thought – and a six-pack of V8 tomato juice. He also had a dozen PowerBars, a nutty-honey-bran sort of thing, and a half-finished plastic bottle of Diet Coke. He had a full sleeve of Oreos – Double Stuf – and two Granny Smith apples. That was all. For eight people and one dog. It didn't amount to much.

They had done a little better with the tools and odds and ends, she saw. They had a hatchet, a pack of fish-hooks, a bobbin of monofilament line, two flashlights, one headlamp, a half roll of duct tape, six tiny airline blankets, a U-shaped pillow – the kind that travelers use on planes – a car jack, a lug wrench, a pair of pliers, a pack of strike-anywhere matches, a jacket from the pilot, a pair of shin-high rubber boots, a pair of thigh-high rubber boots, and six whistles. Those were all the worth-while things, although a knife, she thought, would have been an enormous help. The rest – a messy pile of junk – formed the third pile. It was possible more stuff remained on the plane, but with the water gurgling around and the plane making loud, shuddering sounds, it wasn't going to be easy to find it.

"You guys better not try to eat me," Web said. "I'm not giving anyone permission to eat me if I croak."

"Stop it, Web," Seldon said. "This is serious."

Web looked around with his face broken into a smile, trying to get the others to join in, but no one was inter-ested, E saw.

"Where did Paul and Titus go?" E asked.

"They went back the way the plane came in," Seldon said, "to see if anything valuable dropped out on the way into the crash zone. It's a long shot, but it's worth a look."

"It's going to rain," she said.

Seldon looked up at the sky as if he had forgotten everything but the food and supplies in front of him. Mr. Eliot looked up, too.

"We should get this inside," Mr. Eliot said. "We don't want the food to get wet."

"Titus said we should hang the food," Seldon said. "It could be attractive to bears if we store it inside the hut."

"That kid Suryadi is attractive to bears," Web said. "With his side and everything."

"It's a risk we'll have to run," Seldon said.

Big drops of rain began to fall.

"Grab the ends, and we can drag it inside," Mr. Eliot said. "We can hang it later if we want to. We need to eat something. People are starving."

E grabbed one of the corners and waited until Seldon and Mr. Eliot and Web grabbed the other corners. Then they dragged it to the hut. Rain began falling harder, hitting the ground with tiny explosions.

"Man, look at that," Paul Eliot said.

Titus followed Paul's sight line to the top of the trees. It was obvious how the plane had come through them: the pines bent over in a rough pathway marking the plane's descent, their tops snapped off like icicles from a frozen roofline. It amazed Titus to reconstruct what had happened. At one point, the trees stood unbroken, then the path to the lake began. Obviously, the plane had started down at the point where the first trees dangled. It was simple to see what had happened, because the plane gouged deeper into the tops of the trees as it approached the lake. It had cut the trees on an angle like a wedge of cheese.

"That pilot did a good job to get us to the lake," Titus said, his eyes still on the treetops. "A little lower and we would have been squashed on the tree trunks."

"Those trees are what got him," Paul said, his voice soft and respectful, his eyes riveted to the treetops. "Jenky, too. The branches stabbed right through the plane skin."

Titus nodded. He had thought the same thing.

A few drops of rain began to fall. Titus moved deeper into the woods. It wasn't easy going. Blowdowns and widow-makers – trees that could fall on a logger without warning and make his wife a widow – covered the forest floor. It was rare to find a clear piece for walking once you left the smooth contours of the beach; mostly it was scrambling over one branch, ducking under another, then on and on. But Titus pressed deeper in the forest until he stood directly under what had to be the first snap of trees bent over by the plane's wing and nose.

"Be careful," he said to Paul. "Those tops could drop off anytime."

"Okay."

"Let's just search along the ground. We probably won't find anything, but you never know."

Paul nodded. He inched back toward the beach, his eyes flashing up to see the trees, then back to cover the ground. Titus worked to his right, following the same procedure. Fortunately, they didn't have far to go, because the insects – mosquitoes and black flies – swarmed them. The insects were bad enough on the beach, but here, in the damp shade of the forest, it was unbearable. You couldn't breathe without sucking them into your nose and mouth. Titus remembered reading books about Arctic canoe trips and exploration excursions, but reading about the insects and experiencing them were two different things.

They found the largest part of the right wing a hundred yards toward the beach.

"Not bad," Titus said, circling the wing as much as he could on the uneven ground. "We can use this. It doesn't look too broken up."

"We'll need help carrying it."

"Yep. But if we get enough people, we can get it out. It would make a wicked good roof for something. Maybe we could put it on the hut and make the whole thing more watertight."

The wing rested almost on its end, the top, thicker part, sticking up toward the sky. A few yards farther on, Paul found part of a wheel assemblage. Then Titus uncovered a bunch of glass – from the windshield, from the side windows, he couldn't say – but the rest, bright glitters of plane skin, turned out to be not worth salvaging.

"The wing, that's about it," Paul said when they stepped clear of the forest. The rain had become steadier.

"Everything's worth something," Titus said.

"I get it," Paul said.

Titus wasn't sure who stopped first, but somehow they ended up under a thick tug of pine branches out of the rain. The insects still buzzed in their ears, but somehow it wasn't quite as bad. Titus studied the clouds. The rain wasn't going to lift any time soon. It would sock them in and turn everything damp and slippery. He felt hungry and tired, but he also didn't want to go back to the hut right away. He wasn't sure why.

"What's next?" Paul asked.

Titus shrugged.

"Food's going to be a problem," Titus said. He realized now why he had stopped. He wanted to have Paul as a sounding board. "We can probably figure out how to catch fish. We have fishhooks. But if the temperature starts dropping, we're in real trouble. I doubt we can make ourselves warm enough to survive for long."

"A plane is going to come, though, right? Someone is going to come looking, don't you think?"

"Probably," Titus said. "I mean, of course. The question is whether they know where we came down. If we came down on our projected flight path, then yes, they should find us pretty easily."

"And if they don't?"

"Then we'll have to walk out."

"Do you think we could?"

Titus shrugged again. He didn't know.

"Maybe we could send a party out for help. I don't know. It's dangerous either way. The survival books always say you should stay put and let someone find you. At least that's what I've always read in the Scouts. I know if you get stranded in your car, you usually shouldn't leave it. You shouldn't swim away from a capsized boat unless you're absolutely sure you can make it to shore. But it makes sense to plan for an exploration party, too. You have to figure out all the contingencies."

"I'll go," Paul said.

Titus looked at him.

"It wouldn't be easy," Titus said, sorting it out a little in his mind as he talked. "It would be really, really hard.

And we might not make it. In fact, I would bet we wouldn't make it."

"Would you go?"

Titus nodded. The rain, he noticed, had become a constant drone. He was curious how the hut would hold up to its first rainstorm. He thought it would do okay. It would do better with the plane wing for a roof if he could figure out how to build it.

"You think there are any bears around here?" Paul asked, holding his hand out for the rain. He drank a little of the water from his hand. "For real?"

"I'm sure there are. Grizzlies and black bears. I don't have any doubt."

"That's crazy."

"We probably won't even see one, but you never know. They scout the water's edge, so eventually we'll want to move the camp back. But one thing at a time."

"What else do we need to do?"

"Set up latrines," Titus said. "We've got a million things to do, honestly. It's going to be a lot of work."

"I kind of like it, though, you know?" Paul asked.

Titus looked at him.

"You mean, just kind of the adventure of it?"

Paul shrugged.

"I know what you mean," Titus said. "But it's more serious than that. We can't let it become that."

Titus wasn't sure he had made his point. He wasn't entirely sure what his point might be, exactly, but it had something to do with playing at survival rather than being serious about survival. He knew for certain that any little thing could knock them all down. It wouldn't take much to put an end to them. That was one thing he had gleaned from books about Arctic exploration.

"We should get out of the rain," Titus said eventually. "You don't want to get damp and cold."

"Okay."

"I'm glad we found the wing. And I'm glad we know what's back here. If we hadn't checked, we would have always wondered."

"We can get the wing out."

Titus nodded, then pushed out into the rain. Fog had already covered the lake. The plane, resting with its nose pointed toward shore, looked as though it had passed through a white cloud and had simply lost its way.

The dog was cold, Seldon realized. Or hungry. Or both. He reached down and put his hand on the dog's ribs. *The poor thing*, he thought. It sat in his awkward basset hound way beside the tiny fire, his face forward. Seldon worried the dog's ears might catch fire.

He also worried someone might suggest eating the dog.

Weird, he knew. But possible. If things became too tight, anything was possible. You didn't have to be a survivor guy to figure that out. The entire game had shifted, and now, parked on a beach in a remote part of Alaska, anything was open for discussion. It wasn't likely that anyone would want to eat old Buford, but you never knew.

He reached down and rubbed the dog's chest.

"Can't we have more wood on the fire?" someone asked.

It was hard to tell who spoke in the dimness. Everything inside the hut was cloudy and damp. Smoke lingered near the roof before it passed quietly out, but the rain came in through the opening for smoke and hissed on the hot coals. *Not a perfect system*, Seldon thought. He didn't know what a perfect system might be, but this wasn't it.

At least, though, they were out of the rain. Mostly.

"We need to ration," Jill said, taking up a theme they had been discussing most of the afternoon. "We should come up with a plan to divide the food, then stick to it."

"Anything that can go rotten," Web said, "should go first. We should eat the perishables. It doesn't make sense to hold on to them."

"We need to ration. . . ." Jill said again, but then Paul and Titus ducked into the hut, and the conversation stopped.

"Smoky in here," Titus said. "We need to open the hole in the roof a little more."

"It has no draw," Walter Eliot said from his spot on the opposite side of the fire from Seldon. "The air doesn't move from the bottom to the top."

Seldon watched Titus study the situation. Then he moved to the beach side of the hut and tore out a hole in the side of the wall, down near the bottom. Almost immediately, the smoke began moving better. Air came in through the side, ran forward toward the fire, then followed the heat up toward the ceiling. If you sat low enough and stayed back from the fire, the smoke wasn't too bad now. Titus was a pretty impressive kid when you came down to it, Seldon thought.

"We're talking about food," Walter Eliot said, explaining the topic to his son and Titus. "Everyone's hungry."

"So let's eat," Web said.

"It's a question of how much to eat," Seldon said. "That's the sticking point."

Titus sat down on the bench of sand that ringed the hut. So did Paul. For the first time, really, they were all together. For the first time since the accident, for the first time since they had buried the two bodies. That had been a moment, too, Seldon reflected, but they hadn't talked then. That had been a dark, sad moment. Afterward the different teams had gone about their various jobs, but now, as the sun began setting, they were in the hut sitting around a tiny fire. The flames gave off a haunted look. Jill was the most haunted of all, Seldon thought, except for Suryadi, who no longer spoke. Suryadi was in a bad way, but there wasn't much anyone could do about it. Everything had happened very fast and was still happening fast. It was difficult to slow anything down.

"We've done okay for the first full day," Titus said. "We should all be pretty proud of ourselves. It hasn't been easy."

"I'm starving!" Web said.

Web looked around, and when no one agreed or rallied to what he'd said, he muttered, "I am," then shut up.

"We have shelter," Titus said, "such as it is. We have fire and fuel. It's true we're short on food, but we can manage for a little while. What do people think about aiming at five hundred to a thousand calories?"

"Per day?" Walter Eliot asked.

Titus nodded.

"That's not much," E said.

"We don't have much," Titus said. "We can increase it if we can catch some fish. . . ."

"I hate fish," Paul said, then shrugged.

"We might be able to supplement it somehow. And we have the crossbow. . . ." Titus said. "Maybe we could hunt something."

"Is Titus in charge of everything?" Web asked. "I mean, just because he says something, is that the way it's going to be?"

"Titus is doing great," Seldon said, his hand on Buford, his tolerance for Web shrinking by the minute. "So far, he's been the most useful member of the team."

"We could be in the plane and out of all this rain," Web said, "if anyone ever listened to me."

"The plane is filled with water," Jill said. "And it's creepy in there anyway."

"If we can eat, we will all feel better," Walter Eliot said reasonably. "We should have a meal."

Titus nodded. E, who sat closest to the blue tarp with all the belongings bundled into it, spread the food out on top of the pile. Seldon felt a nervous flutter in his stomach over how little food they had. It was paltry for one person, never mind for eight. He also realized everyone stared at the food as if worried it would get passed out and they would miss out on something. He massaged Buford's ears between his fingers. Buford nosed the tarp, sensing the food.

"The dog's hungry," Seldon said, deliberately keeping his voice level. "Buford is, I mean."

"We're not feeding the dog," Web said. "No way."

"We are, too," Jill said. "He can have my share if it comes to that."

"No one can give away a share," Walter said. "That's something I'll insist on. Everyone has to eat every day as long as there's food."

"What about Suryadi?" E asked.

"Has he been conscious?" Walter asked.

"Not for a long time."

Seldon forced himself to ask the next question.

"Is he still breathing?"

Jill looked over at him quickly, then turned back to the group.

She nodded.

"He's still breathing," she said. "But he doesn't look good. I don't know what we can do with him."

"Keep him comfortable and try to keep him warm," Titus said. "That's all we can really do under the circumstances."

"No first aid kit on the plane?" Jill asked.

"Not yet," Paul said. "We'll look again tomorrow. There's probably some stuff under the water."

E separated the food into piles. PowerBars, sandwich, V8 juice, Double Stuf cookies, apples. She put the half bottle of Diet Coke next to the V8 juice. Liquids with liquids.

"Food is going to be a priority tomorrow," Titus said, standing for a second to examine the supply. "We're going to have to figure out a way to catch fish. Anyone know how to fish?"

"I can," Jill said.

When she saw people looking at her, she continued. "My dad is super into fly fishing. I know how to fish."

"Okay, then you're in charge of fishing," Titus said.

"I can do it a little, too," Seldon said. "I fished as a kid."

"Then you two should work together," Titus said. "That's good. It's good to have two people on a team."

Suryadi made a low, horrible moan. At the same moment, the rain fell harder in a deep, hurried wave. The fire sizzled. Walter Eliot reached forward and put two sticks into the flames to keep them busy.

"We should eat the apples and the ham sandwich," E said, examining the food. "They're the most perishable."

"And an Oreo or two," Web said. "Get real."

"We might need them down the road," Paul said.

"What road?" Web said, his voice suddenly animated, his eyes going around the group. "Listen, if you think we're going to survive for more than a week or two out here, think again. It's not happening! If a plane doesn't come for us, we're goners anyway. A couple Double Stufs either way won't make any difference. Trust me on that."

"Quit being so negative," E said, looking up from the food.

Then Jill stopped them all.

"He's not breathing," she said about Suryadi. "He's not breathing at all."

PART TWO
CAMP LOLLIPOP

I n an extreme situation, you might find water by watching animals at sunrise or sunset. Animals require water, too, so they go to drink at least twice a day. Plot their direction and follow it. Insects — especially mosquitoes — live within four hundred feet of water. If insects assault you, chances are water is nearby.

CHAPTER 7

U sing a sharp, hand-shaped stone, E scored a line in
the calendar pole, making a vertical slash to mark
the twelfth day. The pole had been Web's idea, and
it wasn't a bad one. On one of his reconnaissance walks,
Paul had found the bare branch, stripped off all bark, and
leaned it against the side of the pine hut when he
returned. Web had grabbed it and brought it inside and
had marked off the first three days, counting backward
with everyone's assistance until he came up with the
correct measure. Three days. That was nine days ago, E
realized as she leaned it back against the wall. It looked
like a yardstick or one of those things your parents used
to record your height through your childhood. Something
like that. Web had spent one whole evening scraping in

the legend at the bottom. DAYS UNTIL RESCUE, he had written in stunted block letters.

The truth behind the stick was that time had become hazy. Everyone felt it. Web had been correct about that. Without electronic devices, clocks, cell phones, and computers, it was hard to know what day it was, never mind what time. The days bled into one another, and before you knew it, you could not recall if such and such happened yesterday, or the day before, or maybe even five days earlier. Nothing marked the days except random events, so certain days became the day we found the bear's footprint, or the day the plane flew over, or the day of the first fish.

Or the day Suryadi stopped breathing.

Twelve days. Twelve nights.

But today, at least, was perfect. The weather had dawned sharp and crisp and clear. During the night, it had frosted higher in the mountains, and the morning sun set everything glistening. A pale, scattered frost had touched down on the beach, too, and E had heard Titus and Paul and Mr. Eliot remarking that the insects were not so bad. Not bad at all. The frost had killed them, at least a good portion of them, and that was an enormous relief.

E nearly hit her head on the lip of the plane wing that Titus and Paul had found in the woods. It was now engineered into the roof, and it was a vast improvement over the pine thatch they had had before, because it shed the majority of rain and wasn't such a risk with the fire in the center of the hut. Still, though, she came close to hitting her head every time she ducked under it. She was too tall for hut life.

Camp Lollipop, she thought as she stepped clear of the doorway. It looked pretty good.

It was called Camp Lollipop because Web had found six enormous bags of lollipops in the plane on one of his scouting missions. They had been pushed back under a bunch of maps in one of the overhead compartments, destined, they had guessed, for a school or classroom somewhere in the backcountry. The lollipops had become *the thing*. Everyone ate lollipops all day long. Eventually they would run out, but the consensus had been that the lollipops were essential for morale. They provided something to chew and suck, and when it came right down to it, that was important. Extremely important. So now everyone walked around with a lollipop in her or his mouth, and it was sort of funny, and sort of pitiful, but necessary, also. They worked as a currency, too. You could give someone a lollipop for a favor or the performance of a chore. Each person had a supply, and some people ate them as quickly as they came to them, and others – Jill, for one – chewed on the stick all day and refused to be hurried.

"Nice day, huh?" Mr. Eliot asked.

He sat on a stump near the signal fire. He had a lollipop in his mouth. He was on heaven watcher duty. That was the name they had given to the person selected to keep an eye on the sky in case a plane or helicopter came past. He had two mirrors beside him, both pried free from the plane's bathroom. If a plane came during the day, the heaven watcher was supposed to flash it with a reflection. If it came at night, he or she was supposed to light the signal fire. They had all agreed on the importance of having a heaven watcher.

"It's beautiful," E answered, looking around at the camp. "Where is everyone?"

The heaven watcher also provided another service: He or she was the check-in point for everyone in the camp. If you were going off, you told the heaven watcher. The heaven watcher then knew where everyone was at any point in the day. At night, you simply didn't go anywhere. Especially since the discovery of the bear tracks down by the water on day five.

"Web is in the plane, as usual. And I think Paul and Titus are off scouting or dragging in wood. They're together down at the south end of the beach. Jill and Seldon are fishing. Buford is with them."

"I slept late."

"You must have needed it. What team are you on today?"

"I don't know. Wood gathering with Web, I think. I need to take a swim at some point. I'm filthy, but I suppose I should wait until afterward."

"Titus said people should think about doing laundry today. It's the first truly sunny day we've had in a while."

"We should air out the blankets, too. I'll do that now."

She ducked back in the pine hut and pulled out the small airline blankets they had taken from the plane.

They were thin and nearly useless, but they were all they had for warmth at night besides their clothes. She carried them to the hanging line and threw them over, one by one, until they rested in the sun, arranged neatly down the string. Another Titus suggestion: a group clothesline for hanging laundry or anything else that needed to be off the ground. Web had found the rope for the clothesline underneath the pilot's seat. Little by little, the camp had become more comfortable.

"Would you mind taking the heaven watch for a few minutes?" Mr. Eliot asked when she came back. "I need to use the bushes."

"Go ahead."

"Be right back."

He stood and walked off toward the men's latrine. The women's latrine was in the other direction. Neither latrine was much to brag about, but Titus had recommended they consolidate their waste. That way, he said, they would be less likely to contaminate the drinking water. The latrine was not her favorite place, and she visited it as infrequently as possible.

She sat on the stump Mr. Eliot had occupied and

stared absently up at the sky. Nothing. Only once had they spotted a plane far to the west. It had suddenly appeared on the horizon on day six, maybe two hand-spans higher than the trees when you looked at it, and it appeared to be a commercial jet. They had flashed it, but the sun was dull that day, and the plane was far, far away. Still, it had sent an electric jolt through everyone, and that night they had decided to have a regular heaven watcher on duty at all hours. Everyone agreed it was the best chance at rescue.

On a day like today, E reflected, heaven watcher was the best duty going. You got to sit in the sun and simply watch. It wasn't heavy lifting, but it could be a tad boring if everyone else went away. She let the sun warm her bones. Paul and Mr. Eliot had been correct: The insects were no longer a serious issue.

"Back," Mr. Eliot said.

He held out a lollipop for her. She took it as payment. It was orange. She stood and let him take her place.

He fished another lollipop out of his breast pocket and unwrapped it.

"It's getting cold, huh?" Mr. Eliot said, sitting.

"Not too bad."

"At night, I mean."

"Well, sure, it's pretty cold."

"What do you think about the plan?"

E could think of two plans floating around Camp Lollipop. One was to build stone hives in the woods. Titus and Seldon had already built a small one to try it out. Seldon had seen the hives on a trip to Ireland. They were common in prehistoric settlements, though Seldon was quick to add that it was a whole lot warmer in Ireland than it was in Alaska during the winter. Still, stone hives would protect them from animals, and they would hold heat better than the pine hut.

That was one part of the plan. To build or not to build.

The other part was whether to leave or not. Or to send off a rescue party.

"You mean the building or the rescue party?"

"The building isn't very controversial," Mr. Eliot said. "I think if people want to build, they should build. It wouldn't hurt anything. I mean the rescue party idea. I've got to tell you, I think it's crazy."

E shrugged. She wasn't sure.

"I see the point of it," she said. "We've been here twelve days, and we've only seen one plane. And that was a commercial jet."

"You don't think they're looking for us?" Mr. Eliot asked, his voice a tiny bit shrill. E knew he could become agitated if you disagreed with him about their chances of being found by a plane. He clung to that idea more than anyone else. She phrased her next words carefully.

"I didn't say that. I don't know. I think they *were* looking for us. I just don't know if they're *still* looking for us. In a serious, determined way, I mean."

"Of course they are! I mean, an entire television show just disappeared! We're probably national news."

"We're a small television show on a small channel. I don't know, Mr. Eliot. Sometimes I think leaving makes sense. It's going to get cold soon. Really cold."

He bit down on his lollipop, cracked it, then pulled another out of his pocket. It was purple. He unwrapped it and stuffed the wrapper into the logs on the signal fire. She didn't like how quickly he got annoyed when this topic came up. Still, she found his bullheadedness annoying. A little part of her wanted to puncture his balloon.

"Walking out doesn't make much sense, if you ask me. We could be miles from anywhere," Mr. Eliot said.

"Or not. We don't know, that's the thing. Paul and Titus found the outlet of the lake. We can follow the water downstream."

"Do you have any idea what that country's like?"

"Harsh," she said. "Desolate. No one is saying it would be easy. Especially not Titus. But he says you have to make a decision and stick to it. We can't stay here all winter, that's certain. We'd never make it. And the sooner we leave, the more strength we have for the journey."

"I'm sick of Titus. He thinks he's always right."

"Well, sorry you feel that way. I think he's been pretty awesome."

Mr. Eliot didn't say anything. He looked tired, and his eyes looked empty. Despite what she had been feeling a moment before, she also experienced a wave of compassion for him. He hadn't chosen to be marooned on a beach in Alaska, she reflected. He just wasn't very good at it, that's all. He didn't have the temperament or the stamina. He was a worrier, but mostly he worried about the wrong things.

E took a moment to straighten her posture. Her posture was a constant battle, but she had become sloppy about it while living on the beach. She straightened her shoulders and felt better almost immediately.

"Someone is going to show up," Mr. Eliot said, fluttering the lollipop in his mouth. "That just makes sense. When they do, we better all be here."

"I see both sides," E said.

"I'm staying here."

"That's your prerogative. Everyone has to make an independent decision."

"My son is staying, too."

E nodded. She knew Paul had already talked about leaving with Titus, but she didn't want to raise that with Mr. Eliot for the time being. The day was too nice to spoil with bickering.

"Tell you what, I'm going to take a swim and clean off. Then I'll start dragging in wood."

"Where are you swimming?"

E pointed toward the north end of the beach. Away from Paul and Titus and away from the fishing team.

Mr. Eliot nodded.

"Okay," he said and cracked down on his lollipop. He shoved the empty stick in the pile of signal-fire logs and waved to her as she walked off.

Jill teased the caterpillar forward, feeling the slow tick of the gravel on the fishhook. The caterpillar, skewered on the hook, entered the perfect strike zone. She and Seldon had already caught two fish, both of them fourteen inches or better. She wanted another.

Seldon watched beside her. Buford watched beside him.

"Right there," Seldon whispered.

"We may have fished it out for now."

"No, there should be more."

The strike zone consisted of a seam of fast water that gave way to a backward eddy. The water came in from a stream and curled around a large rock situated in the middle of the outflow. Trout hid around the rock, dodging out to pick off insects and whatever else the stream brought them. Most days, Seldon and Jill used caterpillars or grasshoppers they found back in the woods. The trout didn't seem to have a preference for one over the other. Some days grasshoppers, some days caterpillars. It all depended on what they could find.

She felt a quick tug on the line, then nothing.

"Easy," Seldon whispered.

Jill nodded. She was the best angler, she knew. Seldon was okay, but she was better. She had a feel for it.

A trout hit the line again, and this time she jerked up quickly to set the hook. The water around the rock exploded with the fish dancing on its tail. She didn't try to play it. She simply walked backward quickly, letting the fish slide in through the shallow water and then onto the bank. Seldon bonked its head with a rock. The trout quivered twice, and Seldon hit it again. The trout lay quietly while a trickle of blood dribbled out of its mouth.

"A good one," Seldon said, bending over it to remove the hook.

"Once this water freezes, they won't be in here."

"I know. But one day at a time."

Jill wound up the slack on a piece of wood once Seldon tossed the hook to her. The fishing line stayed on the original bobbin that they had found in the plane. They had thought about dividing the line into two or even three parts, but they did not want to risk so many hooks at once. They had already lost four hooks; they had six more, and then they were in all kinds of trouble, Jill knew.

"What do you say, buddy?" Seldon asked Buford. "You want some fish heads?"

"It's so gross," Jill said.

"No one else wants to eat the heads."

"It's still gross."

Seldon put the last fish beside the others on a long, flat stone they had dragged there for this particular purpose. He didn't have a knife but used a sharpened rock instead. He had chipped it and sharpened it as best he could and had wrapped tape around it for a handle, but it was still grisly to watch him saw through the throat of the trout. He chopped off all three heads, then put them on a second rock that had become Buford's dish.

"There you go, buddy," he said.

Buford came forward and nosed them. Then, almost reluctantly, he began to lick harder.

"We should cook them at least. Roast them over a fire," Jill said. "The poor pooch."

Seldon shook his head.

"Better nutrition to eat it raw."

"But way gross."

"Buford needs to eat, just like anyone else."

Seldon reached out and ran his hand down Buford's back. The dog paused, apparently wondering if his food was being threatened, and Jill saw the tiniest glimmer of teeth under the dog's flappy jowls. Seldon laughed. He took his hand away, and Buford began eating again.

"What a tiger," Seldon said about Buford. "Everyone's channeling an inner tiger around here."

Paul and Titus came up as Seldon finished gutting the three trout. He gave the guts to Buford, too.

The boys were armed with the crossbow and a sharpened spear. Titus carried the crossbow. Jill knew they had been hunting. They hunted often but had not brought anything down yet.

"Anything?" Seldon asked.

The boys squatted next to the fish.

"No, but we saw more bear tracks. We should police the area after Buford eats," Titus said, leaning the crossbow against a rock. The crossbow pointed up at the sky. "Bears can smell fish like this for miles."

"I'll splash some water around," Seldon said.

"Three today?" Paul asked.

"We might get more this evening," Jill said. "We don't want to lose too many hooks."

"Good thinking," Paul said, his hand out to touch the fish lightly. "We need a sauce pot in the worst way. If we could make a soup, the food would go a lot further."

"Web's been all over the plane?" Seldon asked. "No one has found a knife, either. That's bizarre. There must be a knife on board somewhere."

The knife was a genuine piece of Camp Lollipop lore. Everyone agreed there had to be a knife somewhere, but no one had found it yet.

"Web almost lives in the plane," Titus said. "He's always in the plane."

It was true, Jill knew. Lately, Web had been constructing a sleeping platform with pine boughs on top of the seat backs. It was a little weird and a little . . . animal-like, she thought. Like an animal building a nest.

"If we could find a pot," Paul continued on his line of thinking, "we could make a soup and get more from the fish."

"Bones and everything," Titus said.

"Maybe we can manufacture something," Seldon said. "Maybe we could bend some of the plane skin into a pan of some sort."

And that was where the conversation stood when they heard the whistle begin blowing. It blew over and over again, sending out a general alarm, and Jill rose to her feet and looked toward camp.

The heaven watcher's whistle, she knew. She started running almost before she knew what she was doing.

Walter Eliot tried to get the barb of light trained on the plane. It was a small plane, not easy to hit with a ray of sunshine, and it had already passed to the west and south before he had realized it *was* a plane. For a moment, it had been a simple sound, a drone buzzing the sky, and anyone in a civilized place would have let it pass unnoticed. Planes traversed the sky every day, he realized, and you never paid attention to them.

That was what he thought as he came out of his reverie and realized the plane was there, here, now. It was just above him, and he reached and blew the whistle. He blew it long and hard, and it was while he was blowing it that he realized he had reversed the order.

Use the mirror first, then blow the whistle.

That would be the proper order. That was the smartest way to go. The plane couldn't hear a whistle, but it could sure see a reflected light.

But his nerves felt jumbled and crazy and he understood in a deep, horrible place inside him that he had . . .

. . . been asleep.

He had dozed off in the warm sunshine. Then suddenly, the plane was past him, heading south toward hotels and food and warmth, and he had snapped awake when the plane was at the farthest edge of their bowl of sky.

He was still flashing the mirror when Paul and Titus arrived. Seldon and Jill arrived a moment later.

"Did you get it?" Seldon yelled, skidding to a stop. "Did they see you?"

Walter Eliot kept flashing the mirror.

"Did they see you? They must have passed right overhead, Dad."

That was his son. His son had asked that.

Walter kept flashing the mirror.

"Sometimes they wiggle their wings if they see you," Titus said. "Did they wiggle their wings?"

Walter shook his head no.

No, they didn't wiggle their wings.

"They're probably too far away now," Jill said. "They're miles away now."

"It was a small plane, too," Titus said, his eyes up at the sky. "The kind that would be in a search party."

"I don't know if they saw us," Walter Eliot said.

He continued flashing the mirror, but it no longer mattered to him where the spear of light bounced.

"They'll radio our position," Seldon said, his tone tentative. "Right? Isn't that right?"

"It's hard to know if they saw us," Walter Eliot said.

"I bet they heard the report about us, so they would have been looking," Jill said. "Everyone's probably looking."

E came up to the group then. Her hair dripped, and she had obviously been swimming.

"What's going on?" she asked, her breath shaky, her hand holding her ponytail and wringing it out. "Did a plane see us?"

"Hard to say," Walter Eliot said.

What he thought was: *I was asleep.*

"What are you saying?" Seldon asked as Walter Eliot put down the mirror. Walter sat down on the heaven watcher's stump. Seldon stepped closer and bent over to see his eyes.

"I'm not saying anything," Walter explained, feeling annoyed at their questioning. How could he know for sure what the plane saw or didn't see? "I just didn't see them acknowledge us. That's all."

"They would have wiggled their wings," Titus said, apparently puzzled that they hadn't.

"They must have seen us," Paul said. "They flew right over us."

"Hey, where's Web?" Jill asked. "Didn't he hear the whistle?"

Walter was relieved to see the attention switch away from him. He put the mirror down where it was stored against the heaven watcher's stump.

"He was in the plane last I knew," Walter said. "He's always in the plane."

"But they saw the mirror flashes, right?" Titus asked. "They had to. On this kind of day . . ."

"I'm going to go check on Web," Paul said. "He must have heard the whistle."

"I'm sure he heard the whistle," Walter Eliot said, remembering the one thing he had done well. "I blew it like crazy."

Paul went up the side of the plane as nimbly as he could. He had come through the water quietly, and now he scrambled up soundlessly, trying to catch Web at whatever Web was doing.

Because Paul knew Web was up to something.

He didn't know what, and he didn't know why, but his suspicions were raised. He knew Web better than anyone else on *Junior Action News Team*. He had played video games with him, and talked about zombies with him, and had hung out with him in the hotels when they were able to get movies on the pay-per-view channels. He knew Web wasn't building his little nest in the plane for fun. Web didn't do fun that way. The fact that Web hadn't come when the whistle blew confirmed everything. So Paul went up the fake ladder and stuck his head in the opening of the plane, and he saw Web scrambling to put something away.

"What are you doing?" Paul asked, climbing forward. "Web, I know you're doing something, so what is it?"

It was dark inside and hard to see.

But Paul heard crinkling. Like wrappers being crumpled away.

"Are you . . . Do you . . ." Paul asked, climbing into the plane's belly. "What are you . . ."

"Shhhh," Web said.

Web slammed one of the overhead compartments closed. He had just hidden something away.

That's when it began to make sense.

"You have food, don't you?" Paul asked, his voice rising in amazement.

"Shhhh."

Web had built a nest, true enough, from pine boughs and scraps of wood. It was a wide platform near the back of the plane, not far from the overhead compartment where he had hidden the food. Paul found he couldn't really speak or think of what to say because he was so furious.

"We can split it," Web said, his voice coming from the back of the plane. "It's nothing great."

"You're keeping food for yourself? Keeping it from the group? I can't believe it!"

"They didn't want to come in the plane and look. I found it. No one else. I found it, and it's mine."

Paul crawled down the pine platform headfirst and opened the overhead compartment. He had to reach back and down a little behind the shelf, down into a secondary compartment. His hand closed on something – it felt like a sleeve of crackers and a jar of some sort – and then suddenly Web attacked him.

It almost didn't seem real. Web slapped at his arm, making him drop whatever he had held a moment before, and Paul shot his knee up and tried to gouge it into Web's ribs.

But Web was heavy. Paul felt his wind leaving him as Web pressed on him and kept him away from the overhead compartment.

"What, are you going to kill me?" Paul hissed. "Is that what you want to do?"

"It's mine."

"I'm going to tell everyone. That's all there is to it."

"It's not theirs. It's mine. I found it when no one else wanted to look."

Paul pretended to relax. That sometimes worked. When you were a small kid, and a nerdy one to boot, sometimes playing possum worked. You went limp, and fairly often, the other kid gave up. Then you could squirt away. Paul was a master of it, but he didn't know if Web would fall for it. Web was a nerdy, unathletic kid himself. He probably knew most of the tricks.

For a weird moment, they lay together, inhaling and exhaling almost in unison.

"Get off me," he said finally in a firm, flat voice, and Web did.

"We're not friends anymore," Paul said. "We're done."

"Are you really going to tell them?" Web asked, pulling back and retreating to his dark corner. "It's just some peanut butter and crackers. It's no big whoop."

"I can't even talk to you," Paul said, slowly pulling himself toward the door. "I don't even want to see you."

"Go ahead, then," Web said, his voice suddenly defiant. "See if I care."

Paul tried to think of something to say, but nothing came to mind. He scrambled across the pine platform and then out the open door. Then the sun blinded him when he finally sat on the edge of the door frame, looking back at camp. He didn't know what he'd gain by telling the other members of the party, but he also didn't know if keeping Web's secret involved him in it. It was strange all the way around. It was especially strange to think of them wrestling on the pine boughs, down in the darkness like two wild animals.

CHAPTER 8

Which way would you go?" Seldon asked.

"West. Southwest, probably," Titus said. "We'd follow the river. We've been over this a hundred times."

"I just want to go over it one more time," Seldon said. "Humor me. I need to act like an adult a little. It's my job. Someday, someone may come along and ask about what went on here, and I want to be able to answer that I did what had to be done. So tell me again."

"Paul, E, and I," Titus said, his voice practiced with repetition. "We'd leave soon, in the next day or so. We'd take the crossbow for protection. We'd take some matches, too, and the usual camping materials. We can make horseshoe packs out of our blankets. I know how to do that. We'd be near water, so we wouldn't need to carry it. We'd walk seven days, one week, in that direction. No more. If we didn't get anywhere or find anything, we'd turn around. That's about it."

Seldon nodded. He had to hand it to the kid: The plan made sense. It was compelling in its simplicity. Titus did not promise to bring help or find a homestead. He simply promised to try, and it was hard to argue with that given their circumstances.

Seldon looked at the other faces through the wood smoke inside the pine hut, trying to read them. It was tribal meeting time. Web had scraped another notch in the calendar pole. Seventeen days had passed since the crash, and the temperature outside the hut had gone to the other side of freezing. Food supplies had shrunk to near zero. Nothing about their situation had improved in the past week or more.

"You're staying with me," Walter Eliot said to his son, Paul. "That's the last word on it."

"We may all die if he stays," Jill said. "You can't say one way or the other. Everyone has to choose."

"I'm his father."

"I'm going, Dad," Paul said softly. "If the group decides an exploration party is a good idea, I'm going."

"He's proven himself over and over," E said from the other side of the fire, her face blended in smoke. "He's good at this stuff. Almost as good as Titus. And he's in good condition. Almost as good as I am. I'm not bragging; I've just been a dancer all my life, so I'm in shape. Paul should be one of the three."

"Then why shouldn't everyone go?" Web asked. "I mean, at least theoretically. If help is out that way, why don't we all go?"

"We'll travel faster with just the three of us," Titus said, his voice serious and obviously fleshing out thoughts with which he had wrestled. "We'll cover more ground as a small party, and we will need less food. We'll take some of the fish jerky Jill made. But we're going to require some serious calories, and it's harder to provide for six people than for three."

"He's got a point," Paul said from his spot next to Jill. "You know he does. Honestly, we've been over all this. At this stage, we're not really asking for permission anymore. We're saying what needs to happen."

"Who made you king of the world?" Web asked, his voice covered with scorn.

He still had the calendar pole across his lap. He used the sharp end to massage Buford's rump.

Nobody responded to Web, Seldon saw. Web didn't count for much after the news about the stashed food came out. Seldon had a hard time tolerating the kid's presence in the pine hut. But the kid had a thick skin, for sure. Rhinoceros skin. Knowing everyone hated him didn't seem to make a difference to Web.

"We should leave tomorrow," Titus said. "The longer we delay, the colder it will be for us and for the people who stay. We're not getting any stronger, any of us. If we don't make it to civilization, we can come back and be in the exact same situation we're in now. I don't see a downside."

"You could die out there," Mr. Eliot said, his voice drifting into the fire. "Or get lost. A thousand things could happen."

"Better to try than to sit and wonder about it," Paul said. "It just is. And once it starts to snow, we probably can't walk out no matter what. So if we're going to try it, we need to start soon."

No one said anything for a little while. The fire continued to flicker. Outside, the sun had already set. The interior of the hut had become blue with the combination of the last light and smoke. Seldon looked down at his shoes. He had duct-taped them twice already, trying to keep them together. He had even taken to wearing the rubber boots around – the short pair, not the long pair – but they had proved too heavy for everyday use. His good loafers had sprung out at the seams. It seemed years, rather than weeks, since he had bought them.

"I'm going with you," Walter said. "You should have an adult along."

"Why?" E asked.

"If Paul's going, then I want to go, too," Walter Eliot said. "I'm not letting my boy go off by himself."

"I should go instead," Seldon said. "We need an adult here. That only makes sense. I'm younger than you and in better shape. And I can fish nearly as well as Jill. They're going to need fresh fish. We have to be clinical. We can't be emotional about this."

"I won't be separated from my boy," Walter said. "I'm going to go no matter what, so you might as well stay here, Seldon. I know I'm not very good at this survival stuff, but he's my son, and I refuse to be separated from him. That's not negotiable."

Seldon passed his eyes around the circle. No one seemed prepared to speak against Walter's inclusion in the discovery party. Seldon gave the man credit. He didn't blame him for not wanting to be separated from his son. It made sense, too, that an adult should remain behind, so Seldon accepted that role.

"Tomorrow," Walter said for emphasis. "First light. I'm in."

Web slept on his pine platform in the plane. It was cold and wet, but at least he didn't have to deal with the idiots from Camp Lollipop. Besides, the hut was cold and wet, too — wetter, really, than the tube of the plane. He had been inside the pine hut in a hard rain, and it hardly offered any protection besides the outline of the aluminum wing. The plane, on the other hand, was at least out of the rain. Showed how much they knew.

He rested on his back and felt his stomach. He was hungry. He was always hungry now, his stomach a burning little engine revving and cooling under his belt line. He had lost weight, actually, and his hands sometimes roamed to his hips, where he could feel his hip bones sticking out a little through his chubbiness. Not bad. That was one benefit, probably the only benefit, of the crash. He felt fitter than he had in years, maybe in his whole life. On heaven watch the other day, he had stared into a mirror at his reflection, astonished to see his chin wattle had slipped away and his cheekbones had taken on shape.

But he was hungry.

What he wanted was a cheeseburger. Cheeseburger and fries. No, popcorn, he decided. Popcorn and a soda, a tall, ridiculously large soda with a straw that jabbed in and out of the top hole like a trombone slide. And maybe some Swedish Fish for afterward, the fish stale and a little gummy so you could stick them on your teeth and they looked like tiny red shoes. Definitely Swedish Fish.

Thinking about food made him restless.

He slid out from under his blanket and crawled across the pine platform, then stuck his head out of the opening at the top of the plane. He looked around. He liked looking at Camp Lollipop, observing it from a distance. It looked pretty in the moonlight. And the air smelled good. The scent of the mountains and lake mixed with the pinewood smoke coming from the hut. That wood smoke was the one thing, he thought, he would actually miss if they ever got rescued.

That's what he was thinking when he saw the bear.

But he didn't really *see* it. Not at first. It came along the shore and blended with the shadows and the darkness, and he had to squint to see if he was going crazy. Then, little by little, the bear's shape came out of the darkness. It walked with its head down, its nose sweeping back and forth like a cat's tail when it hunts. Web couldn't determine the species, but he guessed it was a grizzly. It looked big enough to be one.

He scrambled down to the pine bed and shot back up to the opening. He blew the whistle. Whoever was on heaven watch had evidently fallen asleep.

"Bear!" he yelled. "Coming down the shoreline. Over there!"

He blew the whistle again. This time, the heaven watcher blew one, too.

Web nearly laughed when he saw everyone stumble out of the pine hut. Buford started to bellow and howl. They all divided their attention among the shoreline, the heaven watcher, and the plane.

"What was it?" Seldon yelled. "What did you see?"

"A bear. Up that way," Web replied.

"Are you sure?"

"He was coming right toward camp," Web said. "Following the lake right to it."

Now who had the better sleeping arrangement? he thought.

He watched a small party go off up the shoreline, a flashlight swinging every which way. He could see just enough to spot the crossbow. That meant it was jerk-head Paul and jerk-face Titus leading the charge. The cool kids. It was weird to think of Paul as a "cool kid," because he had been such a geek, such a wannabe zombie-hunter, and a tiny glimmer of Web missed the Paul he used to joke around with. Still, it made him sick to see them marching off as if they truly intended to face down a bear with a crossbow. They'd run right to the plane if the bear actually charged them.

"He moved off," Web said in a voice that carried across the water. "You can go back to sleep. It's okay."

"I'm not doing heaven watch if there are bears out," Jill said, her voice loud and angry.

She had been on duty. And she had been asleep, Web knew.

The flashlight squad came back. Then he lost what they were saying in the confusion of voices. The light kept flashing back to the shoreline, then up to the plane.

"There was one," Titus called to him. "We found the tracks."

"I told you there was a bear," Web said, shading his eyes from the flashlight beam. "You think I'm making that up?"

"It's good that you saw him," Walter Eliot said. "Good to alert us."

"I do what I can, boss," he said, which was a line out of a movie, but he couldn't recall which one. Sometimes, he knew, he spoke too many lines from movies. His mother had always told him that.

The group stood around talking for a while. Web almost said good night and headed back to bed when E yelled up to him, asking if he minded if the person on nighttime heaven watch posted him- or herself up in the plane.

"I *told* you we should be up here," he said, his voice betraying his annoyance with them all. "Sure you can. Knock yourselves out."

Then he ducked down into the belly of the plane and crawled back to his sleeping spot. He was almost completely conked out when he heard someone wade through the water, then climb up the ladder, and finally settle on the rim of the plane door. Heaven watch.

CHAPTER 9

In the first light of morning, Paul slipped the horseshoe pack over his shoulder and neck, then adjusted it a little so that it would be more comfortable. It was heavy. Titus had demonstrated how to convert their airplane blankets into packs. You rolled them diagonally, like a crescent-shaped dinner roll, with whatever you wanted to carry inside. Then you knotted them and threw them over your neck. Simple and efficient, but heavy, too. It was not as balanced as a backpack. In the first two seconds he wore it, it began to dig into his neck.

"Ready," Paul said.

He didn't feel particularly ready. What had seemed like an adventure last night now seemed like the craziest idea anyone ever had. It was one thing to contemplate hiking into the wilderness and quite another thing to strap a pack over your back and strike out.

But he wasn't going to back down. Not now.

Web brought the calendar pole and held it over his knee while he scored the first day into the pole. This was a second measuring legend, Paul saw. The larger one – the one that counted all their days – took up most of the space. The second stripe, where the exploration party's journey was notched, was much narrower. Web had scraped in the name they had given to the exploration group at the bottom of the calendar log. They called themselves Team Four, a play on the *Junior Action News Team* name. Last night, Paul remembered, it had seemed like a hilarious name. It didn't seem nearly as funny this morning as he stood with a horseshoe pack hanging around his neck.

"Here," Jill said, stepping forward to hand Titus the fish she had dried and wrapped in a handkerchief. "It won't taste very good, but you'll probably need it."

"Thanks," Titus said.

He slipped the handkerchief in his pack.

It was drizzling a little. The sun had trouble pushing through the clouds.

"We should get going," E said, her pack smoother and neater than his own, Paul saw. "If we're going, let's go."

"One week, promise me," Seldon said. "Then you'll turn back no matter what."

"One week," Titus said. "Remember, though, it will take a week to get back, too. Two weeks total."

"A fortnight," Web said, looking up for a moment from the calendar log.

"And if someone comes in the meantime, you tell them we left to the southwest, following the outlet," Titus said. "Once they know our direction, they can find us in no time."

"And keep up the heaven watch," Walter said.

Walter did not look good. Paul thought his father looked sick. His dad had been in the bushes several times this morning. He had problems with his stomach. That wasn't good, Paul knew from his own experience. They had all experienced it.

"Are you okay, Mr. Eliot?" Jill asked. "You look shaky."

"I won't lie. I'm not great right now. I've got a little belly rumble going on."

"I don't think you should go," Jill said. "If you're not one hundred percent, you shouldn't risk it."

"I'll be okay."

But Paul knew his father. He knew he would not be okay, not this morning, not on the trip. It was crazy to start the journey with a sick person. The fact that his father was not exactly cut out for this type of trip only made it all the more obvious.

"Dad," Paul said, "you can't go. Not feeling like you do. You'll slow us down."

"I'm not letting you go by yourself. How would I ever explain that to your mother if something happened to you? Or to myself?"

"Something already has happened to us, Dad," Paul said, deliberately making his voice soft. "And we're trying to do the best we can. All of us. I promise I won't take any unnecessary risks. I'll be as safe as I can be. But we have to do this, and you need to stay here."

Before his dad could say anything, Seldon stepped forward and took the horseshoe pack Walter had prepared. Seldon slung it over his shoulder and looked around the group.

"I'll go with you," he said simply. "Just a small change of plans."

No one argued. No one tried to talk him out of it. Paul was glad his dad would stay at Camp Lollipop. His dad had no business out on the trail.

Web held up the calendar log for everyone to see. He had marked the first day beside the name TEAM FOUR. He'd done a good job with it.

"Okay, then," Titus said. "Let's go."

He held the crossbow across his chest. They had debated about the advisability of carrying the crossbow. Yes, it provided some security against bears, but it was also heavy and cumbersome to carry. The idea was that they might be able to hunt game with it. Titus said they could come across moose, or maybe even caribou. Paul wasn't so sure it was worth it.

Paul felt his dad's approach more than saw it. The

next thing he knew, his dad had him in his arms and both of them were rocking back and forth. Paul felt all the emotion of the moment numbing his throat and making it hard to breathe. His father kept squeezing and rocking, rocking and squeezing.

"I love you," his dad said finally when Paul managed to slip out of his arms.

"Love you, too, Dad."

Then a surprising thing happened. Jill came forward and hugged him. She hugged him tight. It made Paul feel strange.

"Bye," he said.

"Stay safe and travel well," she said.

He felt the lump go back into his throat.

"And watch out for zombies," Web said. "Get to high ground, remember."

Paul smiled. Then everyone turned to watch Seldon say good-bye to Buford. The dog couldn't go. Buford refused to be consoled and instead kept pushing against Seldon's legs as if that would prevent them from being separated. Seldon had tears in his eyes.

"Hold on to him, would you?" he asked Jill.

They hooked him to a leash. They hadn't been using it at all since the crash, but now they did.

"Don't let him slip his collar," Seldon said to Jill. "He'll try to follow me."

"I'll take good care of him."

Seldon kissed the top of Buford's head, then turned and headed down the shoreline. After a moment's hesitation, Paul followed.

CHAPTER 10

Camp Lollipop felt empty without E, Seldon, Paul, and Titus, Jill discovered. That left only Mr. Eliot, Web, and Buford for her to hang with. In all her calculations about going or staying, that part of the equation had never quite occurred to her. She had always thought about Team Four going off to some unknown destination, and the calculation centered about whether it was better to risk the party or to stay and hunker down the best they could. What she hadn't thought about, what none of them had thought about, was the plain weirdness of being left with Web and a sick Mr. Eliot.

If she had thought it through, she realized now from her station at the heaven watcher's stump, she would have gone with them.

But she hadn't. Part of that was because someone had to stay behind. If a plane or a helicopter had any chance of seeing them, then it would see the downed plane, the signal fire, the mirror flash. It wouldn't see Team Four. Team Four had disappeared in no time, their shapes wavering first in the misty morning sunshine, then trickling away like fire going down a fuse. Then nothing. They might have fallen into the center of the earth for all she knew.

She reached down and petted Buford. He burped almost at the exact instant, and she smelled fish heads and guts. It turned her stomach.

"You're disgusting," she said to Buford.

But she kept petting him. He leaned against her leg. She was still petting him when Web came back from the men's latrine.

"Where's Walter?" he asked.

She shrugged. She tried to talk to Web as little as possible.

"He should tell you if he goes off somewhere," Web said.

"I thought you didn't like Titus's rules."

It was Web's turn to shrug.

"You want to hear something weird?" he asked.

She shrugged. That's what people did when they didn't like each other, she realized. They shrugged a lot.

"I think a wolf pack came by camp," Web said. "I saw some tracks back by the bushes."

"You're kidding me."

"No, I'm not. At first I thought it was Buford. You know, maybe he had left tracks back there. But there were too many tracks for one dog to make."

"You're telling me wolves are watching us at night?"

"Maybe. I don't know. Maybe coyotes. Something canine, though. I can't figure what else would be in a pack like that."

"Are you making this up, Web?"

She studied his face. It would be like him to make up something to terrify her, but his expression didn't give anything away. She supposed it was possible for wolves to stalk them, or at least be curious about them. You couldn't count out something like that.

Before she could say anything, Buford burped again.

"That is rank!" Web said, taking a step away and waving his hand in front of his nose. "That's so bad."

"We need wood," Jill said. "For tonight. Wolves or no wolves, we still need wood."

"What's Walter doing, anyway?"

She shrugged again. Camp Lollipop's discipline had fallen to pieces after Titus's departure three days earlier. She was the only one who brought in food. Even though Mr. Eliot still wasn't one hundred percent, the least he and Web could do was to bring in wood every day, but they didn't. She wondered if they had started to go feral, like pigs down in Arkansas somewhere. Domestic pigs sometimes got away, she knew, and by the third generation, they were wild, crazy things. Maybe, she thought, that was happening to Web. He certainly smelled the part!

She started to smile, thinking about her mean little insult, when something fluttered on the edge of her hearing. It sounded like an electric fan on a hot day, maybe with a piece of paper caught between the blades, but then it grew louder. She cocked her head to one side.

She saw the sound register in Web's expression, too, and both of them, she knew, suddenly understood.

"Do you have the mirror?" Web asked.

She did. She did have the mirror.

She began slowly moving the slanted light up at the sky. The sound grew louder. Walter Eliot blew his whistle from somewhere, but she didn't look to see him. She kept her eye on the mirror, then on the horizon behind them, then back on the mirror. The sound drew closer, and Walter kept blowing his whistle, and she wanted to tell him to shut up, to be quiet, but he kept blowing and blowing and blowing, and then the plane suddenly shot into the sky above them.

She nailed the plane with the reflected light. Over and over she hit it. And the plane had only gone halfway across the lake when it waggled its wings and began circling back, the pilot plainly visible in the cockpit.

Jill screamed.

So did Web.

And then Jill broke into tears.

Δ   Δ   Δ

Web watched the plane maneuver for a landing, its heavy pontoons like a pair of duck feet, its propeller changing sounds as it cut back on its engine.

It was over.

It was suddenly, remarkably, over.

That felt impossible. It was too simple. The human mind, he thought, could not go from gritty despair to such overwhelming joy in the space of seconds. It was too much. He felt his mouth grinning as his lips trembled. His face had a collision of emotions.

Finally, he gave in to it. He put his head in his hands and began crying, too. Big, sloppy sobs. He couldn't help it. Then he felt Jill hugging him, and from behind her, a weakened Walter Eliot weeping and shouting and laughing. Even Buford looked up, his long, stupid face curious about the plane coming closer.

"That's it, that's it, that's it," Walter Eliot said, as though his voice could guide the plane to a safe landing.

But it wasn't needed. The plane splashed down easily on the lake surface and kicked up water as it taxied closer to the shore. The pilot left a respectful distance between his plane and their own shattered one, then he swiveled a little and cut the engine, and before Web could adjust to anything, a man in a black baseball hat stood on the pontoon and waved.

"You the folks from the television show?" the man called. "Must be, right?"

"Yes, sir!" Walter Eliot called. "Absolutely!"

"Well, you've been hiding pretty good. No one's seen a hair of you. Is that all of you?"

"Some others headed out to find help. Four of them."

"You're off the track is why . . ." the man said, and Web realized he was talking about why no one had seen them, not answering Walter.

"Do you have any food?" Web called.

"A little. Just my lunch, really, but you're welcome to it."

The man hopped down into the water. He wore rubber thigh waders. Then he pushed the plane a little closer to the shore. It was all as easy as that. The man looked rugged and small, like a feisty little terrier, Web thought.

"Nice little wickiup," the man said, pointing his chin toward the pine hut. "Pretty cozy in there, I bet."

He threw a rope onto the shore. Then he walked the remaining distance with the rope over his shoulder. It was apparently just to keep the plane from drifting off. It wasn't an anchor, Web realized.

"Jerrod Thomas," the man said, reaching out to shake Walter's hand, then Jill's, then Web's own. "Most people call me Candy."

The man smiled. Web felt the craziness of it all. In minutes, they could hop on the plane and leave Camp Lollipop forever. It made him feel all kinds of ways. He saw that Jill and Mr. Eliot were experiencing similar emotions. It was bizarre. He couldn't sort it out fast enough.

"As I said," Candy went on, "you're a little off the track. That's natural enough. As the crow flies isn't always a precisely straight line."

"Have many people been looking?" Jill asked. "We didn't know. . . ."

She still had tears dripping down her face.

"Oh, my, yes. You've been a feature on the news. They made a general bulletin to any planes traveling in this zone to be on the lookout. You've been a major story for a while."

"Were you looking or just passing by?" Walter Eliot asked.

"I was looking. The network people have three planes out at different times. It took time to cover the ground. Alaska's a big place, and you could have gone down anywhere on the flight line."

Candy bent down and petted Buford.

"This guy made it, huh?" Candy asked.

"Looks like it now," Walter said, his voice folding over in a goofy, strange laugh.

"Well, now, what do you need from here? What do you want to pack up?" Candy said. "We won't likely be out this way again until the spring."

"Nothing," Web said. "Let's just get out of here."

"Wait just a second. Let's look around," Jill said. "There might be some things."

"Where'd you say the other group went?" Candy asked.

Walter Eliot pointed.

"South by southwest," Walter said. "They're following the outflow. My son, Paul, is with them."

"How many? You said four?"

"Four people."

The man made a quick calculation, Web saw. He did the subtraction. He had been looking for ten and had found three. Four more were off somewhere else. The difference was dead.

"I'll radio it in once we get in the air. Not much reception in these valleys. That's rough country they're heading for. How many days ago did they leave?"

"Three days," Web said.

Candy nodded.

"They figured they should make a try at getting out," Jill said.

"Of course they did," Candy said. "Most natural thing in the world."

Walter Eliot didn't know where to put his eyes. The sight of Camp Lollipop dug into his heart each time he looked at it, but he couldn't look away. Not yet. The pilot stood on the pontoon and whistled softly between his teeth as he pushed them away from shore. Jill had insisted on bringing the calendar pole, and the pilot used it to push away, then stuck it in the cockpit without a word. He hopped in afterward and slammed the door shut behind. He kept whistling softly as he did his preflight checklist. Buford snuffled forward to smell the pilot, then backed up awkwardly to sit beside Jill.

Walter Eliot felt empty and joyful and scared. He couldn't sort out his emotions. He stared at Camp Lollipop, wondering how they could simply leave it. They had to, of course, but it still wrenched him to be away from it, to be in a tidy little plane cabin, waiting for liftoff. Other than the calendar pole, they had left everything else, figuring if somehow Team Four made it back to camp, then at least they would have the basics. Jill wrote a note and put it in the pine hut where they couldn't help but see it.

SAVED. PILOT SENDING HELP.
WE WILL FIND YOU! STAY HERE!

Walter had helped her compose the note, and they had both agreed simpler was better. Too many words might confuse things. The main point was to keep them here if they returned. Candy had the coordinates. It was

148

a forty-five-minute hop from Fairbanks, thirty-five with a tailwind. A piece of cake to get them. Candy had said the authorities would laugh when finally they found out how close by the *Junior Action News Team* crash had been.

Waiting for the pilot to start the engine, Walter felt himself tearing up again. More than anything else, he wished Paul had stayed. He had *told* him to stay, that was certain, but Paul had insisted on going. It had been a grave mistake, one Walter had known he was making even as he'd committed it. You stayed with your dad. You stayed with family. You didn't go traipsing off into the woods hoping to find a way out. They hadn't listened, and now he had been proven correct.

But that didn't help his son.

"Guess we're ready!" Candy yelled. "You all want to say good-bye to the place? We could circle around."

"Good-bye," Web said. "See you later! Just get us out of here!"

Walter had to wipe his eyes. Jill, he saw, whispered good-bye.

Then the plane began to move.

"Have you home in a jiff," Candy said, his voice rising

to pass over the mounting engine sounds. "Or if not home, at least to a hot shower and some good chow."

Walter nodded. That sounded good. But it felt like cheating to sit in a plane and feel it begin to skim across the water. It felt like abandoning his son, abandoning them all. They had stuck it out together, and now three lucky members, plus Buford, got to zip away, shoot across the treetops, and leave. He cried harder. He had never felt such a strange mixture of emotions.

"Up, up, up," Web said as the plane began to leave the water. "Up you go."

Then the plane banked and Walter realized they were in flight, no problem, and the lake receded below them like a green-blue coin flipped into a sea of pine trees. He turned in his seat to see Camp Lollipop disappear. He heard Candy open up radio communications with a home base somewhere. He said he had the television people, gave a series of coordinates, then said, in answer to something, "Three."

Three survivors, Walter knew.

"Seven," Walter corrected him. "Seven survivors. And Buford, our dog."

But that claim wasn't certain. Three were certain. The rest, Walter understood, were still not rescued. They were still in jeopardy. They had followed a river toward the west, an area that Candy had said was rough. Very rough. Not to mention the snow called for by the latest forecasts. They had another four days before they would even consider turning back.

"Good-bye," Jill whispered again, and this time, Walter guessed, she meant good-bye to her sister.

Walter reached over and took her hand. To his surprise, Web reached for his hand and held it, too. The plane made a good solid sound of flying, and Candy told the radio everything he knew about them. Walter listened, and at times it seemed the pilot talked about people from a newscast somewhere far away. Survivors. Plane crash. An unnamed lake not far from the old Hubbard Line.

SURVIVAL TIP #3

Making a simple emergency shelter can be as easy as finding a downed pine tree. Make sure the tree is solidly on the ground — pine trees can spring forward or back if they are still green and the limbs are not secure — then decide where the tree is thickest. Gradually break off branches below the trunk so that you create a hole in the tree between the trunk and the ground. Use the broken limbs as a floor for your shelter. Usually, you will have to back into the newly formed slot. If you have a tarp, put it on the ground below you. If you have two tarps, it is easy to spread the second tarp above, using the pine limbs as convenient tentpoles.

CHAPTER 11

It was a mistake.

And now he had added a second mistake to it.

That's what Seldon thought as he came slowly out of the bushes, pulling his belt tight against his empty stomach. He felt empty and drained and garbled in the guts. Whatever Walter had, Seldon knew he now had it, too. Might have been something they ate. Might have been anything at all.

To come at all had been his first mistake.

To leave the Team Four party had been his second.

He felt weak. He *was* weak. His frequent trips to the bushes had sapped his strength. His feet, too, had become two pillows of bloody tissue. His loafers had popped and the duct tape had given way, and he could not take more than a few steps at a time without stopping to rest. Bad footgear. He was essentially walking barefoot.

A mistake to come with the party. A mistake to leave the party. Bad thinking. Panic. Stupid, heroic thinking.

Don't worry, I can make it back alone. It's a day and a half, right? Not that far. I'm sorry I can't continue, but maybe you would make better time . . .

All those words. All those rationalizations. What had he been thinking? It was crazy to head into the wilderness alone. He knew better. What was he trying to prove? It made him angry just to think about it.

And now he stood near the water, the outflow of the lake, and he felt too tired to take another step. He had stupidly ended up in the middle, not one place or another, not at camp or in the discovery party. It had been a fundamental mistake.

Jumping jackrabbits, he thought.

He didn't know where that phrase had come from, but it buzzed around his head like a squirrel rattling up a tree. It had been with him the entire trip.

Jumping jackrabbits.

He leaned on his wooden staff and walked three steps forward. He tripped slightly on the uneven rocks because he could not lift his feet high enough to accept the irregularities in the terrain. He needed to find a place to spend the night. He needed to lie down. If he could just rest for a while, he thought, then it would be okay. He could get his strength back.

He had listened carefully when Titus had talked to him about survival techniques. He had listened, honestly, but hearing Titus talk about it was way different from having to put the techniques into practice. Way different. Titus had said something about sleeping under a downed pine tree, but Seldon wasn't sure how that was supposed to work. He was supposed to back into the tree branches and make a little cave. That was the idea, but it seemed crazy now that he stood on the mucky beach, trying to sort things out.

He looked back down the shoreline. Then he looked up it.

Nothing. Zero.

Jumping jackrabbits.

He took two more steps forward. Then he stopped.

Make a plan, he told himself. *Make a plan and stick to it. Get back to Camp Lollipop. Get there, keep going.*

Before he could move, it started to snow.

It was pretty, actually. It came very softly, quietly, the good kind of snow, the sweet, memorable kind of snow. It reminded him of snow he had known as a boy. The kind of after-school-first-snow-of-the-year sort of snowfall. He remembered how it had smelled, how the snow had tasted on his tongue, how the warm kitchen light had thrown a blade of welcome across the backyard. Yes, he remembered all that from playing out in the snow as a child. Now the snow fell here in Alaska, and he held out his hand and told himself not to get distracted, to get going, to find a tree and back into it. That was what he was supposed to do, but he didn't seem to care about doing it.

He hoped they were taking good care of Buford. He hoped that.

It took him a long time, but eventually he came to a bare tree trunk at the water's edge. It wasn't a pine tree, but he dug under it and made himself a shelter. It wasn't much. He crawled in, and it felt like being an animal, not a human animal but a real, go-to-the-ground sort of animal. A badger, maybe, or maybe a prairie dog. He squeezed down and tried to get completely under it, but it didn't work the way Titus had outlined it. He ended up resting next to it, his shoulder under a portion of the trunk, the snow falling gently onto the beach and disappearing. He pushed a little more and managed to get his head under the trunk, and that kept the snow from his face. An improvement. That was better.

He stayed and listened to the water running by and listened to the late crows calling to one another, and he worried that his legs would freeze with the snow falling on them. He scooped a little beach dirt up onto his legs, but the sand dug into his hands and made them hurt.

Finally, he slept. He went far away, and he remembered coming inside to see his mom warming soup, her head turning to him, the vapor from the boiling pot obscuring her face.

Did you have fun? she asked.

But he couldn't answer. His mouth wouldn't work, and his eyes didn't want to close.

"We can't cross, and we can't float it," E said, her voice low and studied. "This is the end of the trail, partners."

Titus listened, but his mind was on the tactical problem in front of them. E was correct. They couldn't cross, and they couldn't float it. The band of water they had followed from the lake had broadened and strengthened and had knotted together into white rashes of rapids. Now it had surged into a small canyon, or squeeze box, and the banks on either side rose up in flanks of granite or basalt. Not passable. To go over the steep slope would require too much time, he knew. They would have to backtrack, then find an access point, then climb. He couldn't tell how technical the climb might be, but he doubted they had the strength to attempt it. By the time they made it over, it would be time to turn back.

"Doesn't look good," Paul said from his other side. "E's right. We're done."

"We're never done," Titus said reflexively.

It was not good to concede even small defeats. Giving up could become a way of thinking, and you could not let it infect you if you were trying to survive.

"Even if we could build some sort of raft or boat," E said, "it would get smashed in the first hundred yards. You couldn't steer it. You'd be freezing cold in no time, and it's not even certain you could make it anyway. I think we should camp here for the night and turn back tomorrow."

"We could go over land," Titus said.

He didn't really believe it himself, but he had to put it into the mix of options.

"You mean leave the river and go deeper into the woods?" Paul asked.

"I don't know what I mean, really," Titus said, pulling back from his position next to the water. "I'm just thinking aloud."

"It's snowing," E said. "Holy mackerel, it's actually snowing."

Titus looked up. White flakes drifted softly down from a gray sky.

"We should make a camp anyway," Paul said. "We can figure it out once we have a shelter."

Titus nodded. Night would come on even faster given the snow. The snow changed everything. The snow could be a game-over message.

"We can do a lean-to using that rock over there," Paul said. "Easy breezy, apple peezy."

"Okay," Titus said. "Sounds good."

He turned back and looked at the water.

Could he swim it? He couldn't say. He might be able to. He was a decent swimmer. He could fill up his shirt with air or cling to a hunk of wood. He might make it. He could send Paul and E back and continue on himself. It was nuts to even think about it, he knew, but not nuts if you considered that the alternative was to travel back to a camp that was in trouble anyway. Was in big, serious trouble. Truthfully, it seemed to him like a coin toss. You took your chances either way. If he could stay afloat and make it through the rapids, at least as far as it went through the gorge, then he could come out the other side and maybe, just maybe, find something.

Or he could drown.

Or he could simply find more woods and hummocks and marshlands.

"Let's build," he said.

But the water stayed in his head.

He pulled himself away from the water and helped E drag pieces of brush and pine boughs to lean against a rock outcropping. It was a good setup for a lean-to. The rock projected a little back onto the trail, and it was no problem to create a small cave of wood and stone, where they could set a fire and receive the reflected heat of the flames. Not only would the fire keep them reasonably warm, it would also discourage animals. They had seen a million tracks, some of them made by bears, and Titus did not plan to make it easy for a predator to pick them off. The crossbow could do little against a full-grown grizzly, so the trick was to make it seem like a bad idea to attack them before the notion got implanted in a bear's head. That was the beauty of a fire and a lean-to.

With all three working, it took only an hour to get the camp set up. By that time, snow had covered the ground. It fell into the water and onto the pine and brush they leaned against the rock. When Titus finally crawled under to get out of the wind and cold, the tight kernels of snow sizzled on the brush. It was a smaller, narrower sound than the liquid hum of the river.

"That's better," Paul said when he had the fire going. "Much better."

"I hope Seldon got out of the snow," E said. "I'm worried about him."

"He'll make it back. Won't he make it back, Titus?"

Titus shrugged. He wasn't sure. He wasn't sure about much at the moment. He felt dizzy and weak.

"How much fish do we have left?" E asked.

"Only a few bites left," Paul said, taking out the nearly empty bandanna that Jill had given them. "I've never been so hungry in my life. I think we're starving. How do you know when you start to starve? Is there a sign or something?"

"I think I need to swim the river," Titus said, throwing the words out like you would throw grain to chickens. He wasn't sure why he let it pass his lips, but he did, and he waited to gauge their reactions.

"You can't swim that," Paul said, putting more wood on the fire. "That's crazy talk."

"He's right, Titus," E said. "Even if you could make it, you can't be sure it would get you anywhere good. I mean, if there was a city waiting for you just past those rapids, it might be worth it. But you could do the whole thing and end up exactly where we are right now. No food, no body warmth . . . It doesn't make sense. Once you go down that river, you can't come back. You're committed to going all the way out."

"Does it make sense to go back to Camp Lollipop?" Titus asked. "Or starve and freeze here? We're out of options. We're running out of strength."

For a while, no one said anything. Titus glanced at them with sideways looks. They looked tired and dirty and thin. Real thin. He imagined they saw the same changes in him. They wouldn't make it too much longer in Camp Lollipop. Once the snow set in and the lake began to freeze over, it was game over. True game over. They might be able to hang on a little longer, but even that was doubtful. And it wasn't going to be pleasant. It was going to be ugly and horrible. Then what? He couldn't even push his mind to think about it.

He could swim and take a chance. He could think about that.

Paul handed out half of the dried fish. It was disgusting. Titus had to eat it with his mouth open to mix cold air with the horrible taste. He didn't like fish to begin with, and now chewing dried fish skin made him gag. He forced himself to eat. He followed Paul's example of holding the fish out to the fire to warm it slightly before biting it apart. He promised himself that if he did get out of this predicament he would never eat fish again.

He ate trout and thought about the river.

E shivered herself awake. It was late. Or early. She couldn't tell for sure. The night seemed to go on forever. She lay between Titus and Paul, her blanket tight around her, the fire smoking in a lazy, tired way. She sat up and put a little wood on it. The fire refused to catch, so she had to bend and twist and get her lips into a position to blow onto the coals. It still wouldn't catch. She broke off smaller twigs, then stirred the coals until she had a red base. After a few more minutes of blowing, the fire finally returned. She felt light-headed from hunger and from blowing so much air at the fire.

"What time is it?" Paul whispered.

"No idea."

"It feels like morning."

"It's still dark. Keep sleeping if you can."

"I'm too hungry to sleep. I keep waking up."

"I'm awake, too," Titus said from his position on the ground. "Can't really sleep."

"Let's get a good fire going," Paul said. "We'll all feel better with a good fire."

E loaded the fire with wood. It felt good to have the heat and light, and good to have company in the darkest part of the night. They made a good team, she realized. Seldon should not have come with them in the first place. That had been a mistake, but sometimes you didn't know a mistake until it bit you on the ankle. She sent out a little thought beam to Seldon, wishing him a quick trip back to Camp Lollipop. He was a good guy when all was said and done. She wondered how he had spent the night.

"It's cold," Titus said. "How much did it snow?"

Paul crawled to the edge of the lean-to and looked out.

"Four or five inches," he said.

"We should head back at first light," E said.

"Head back to what?" Titus asked. "We have to face it. If we don't go on, we're finished. We'll die."

"You don't know that," Paul said. "You know I respect you, Titus, but you don't know that."

E watched Titus in the firelight. He didn't argue or say anything. She held her hands out to the fire. Snow had come into the lean-to and covered the dirt floor with moisture. It had melted with the fire heat and turned everything muddy and sticky and disgusting. So much of what they had lived through had been disgusting, she reflected. She had become immune to filthiness.

"What's the difference between stuffing and dressing?" Paul asked after a while.

It was a game they played. A game to remember food. E knew Paul started it to get Titus off the idea of swimming the rapids.

"Dressing is outside the turkey, and stuffing is on the inside," E said, happy to change the topic of conversation.

"I like the part of the stuffing that is crusty. It has a little crusty surface, and when you bite into it . . ."

"Does your mother use onions and celery?" E asked.

"Both, I guess. And sometimes apples and walnuts."

"I bet that's good," E said. "What does your mom put in the dressing, Titus?"

He didn't answer.

"Sweet potatoes and regular mashed," Paul said. "With the turkey, I mean."

Paul poked the fire with a piece of wood. E couldn't say for certain, but it felt like morning had come through the snow and settled slowly around them. She couldn't say it was light, but the darkness seemed less defined. Birds had not yet started to call. She liked it when the birds called, because that meant one more night had been endured. They had endured it.

"It's getting light," Titus said.

"The nights are wicked long now," Paul said.

"Pretty soon they'll be longer. They'll be as long as anything," E said.

"It's my decision to make," Titus said. "The swimming, I mean."

"We're in this together," E said, her stomach feeling nervous and empty and spoiled. "We need you at Camp

Lollipop, even if we can't keep going. It's not your decision alone."

No one spoke after that. Paul dug in his pack and came out with the last of the fish. E passed on it. Titus took a little and chewed it loudly. It was disgusting stuff, E thought. If she had to survive much longer by eating dried fish, she wasn't sure she could do it. Paul was the only one who seemed capable of tolerating it. He ate a piece and then pushed out of the lean-to. E heard him go off into the bushes. He came back a minute or two later.

"Lots of tracks in the snow," he reported. "Nothing big, but a lot of animals."

"Probably drawn to the fire and our scent," Titus said.

"Can we make some sort of igloo?" E wondered aloud. "Out of the snow and everything. Do you know how to make one, Titus?"

"Not really. You dig down, same as we did with the pine hut. Then you circle it around with snow blocks. But it depends on the kind of snow you have to work with. I made one once. It wasn't very good."

"It would be warmer, though, right?" Paul asked. "Warmer than the pine hut? More protected?"

Titus nodded. E pushed past them and went out to the bushes. She watched the snow tumble softly from the branches. Despite the snow, it did not feel that cold. It wasn't winter; it was late fall. Most of the three days they had been traveling, they watched birds migrating south. Everything seemed to be moving. Even they had been migrating until they came to the rapids.

When she came back to the lean-to, the boys had pushed down the walls and fed them to the fire. The fire blazed up. E realized there was nothing to cook, nothing to warm. She grabbed her blanket, shook it free of dirt and snow, and wrapped it around her head and shoulders. She looked like a tiny peasant woman, she thought.

"If it gets a little lighter, we can travel," Paul said, his hands out to the fire, his eyes scanning the area. "We might get lucky and come across something to hunt. Deer or something. This is the time of morning they come down to drink, right? I'm right about that, aren't I?"

Titus didn't say anything.

E shrugged her shoulders after an awkward ten count and said, "Probably."

That was when she knew Titus intended to swim the rapids. He didn't have to say anything. She knew he had made a decision.

CHAPTER 12

Web ate his second cheeseburger in six bites. He counted the bites. They were fast-food burgers, brought from someplace – not a national brand – in a white paper bag. The bottom of the bag came loaded with a nest of fries. He had a strawberry milk shake, too, and he found it difficult to stop sucking at the straw long enough to eat. Then, while he was eating, he found he wanted to suck the straw again. The food went in like a squirrel shivering down his belly. He was astonished how good it felt.

While he wasn't eating, he listened to them making plans about finding Team Four.

Rangers. Cops. Mountain men and women, for all Web knew. They all buzzed around the cinder-block building next to the airport, their radios crackling, their equipment set out on cafeteria tables. A hundred different conversations, map coordinates, and so forth. They waited for enough light to fly. They said that over and over again. And the snow had complicated things.

Across the table, Jill sipped at a Diet Coke and finished a small fry. Walter Eliot had already eaten and had gone off with a few of the men to look at maps. That was a joke, Web reflected. Walter wasn't exactly the guy to put you onto the correct trail.

"I'm stuffed," Web said, finally pushing the milk shake away. "Amazing."

"Don't eat so much, then," Jill said.

She ate a fry in six bites. The same amount of bites Web had used to eat the second burger.

"I can't believe you're not eating more," Web said. "Aren't you starving?"

Jill didn't say anything. She mostly stared out the security window from where they sat. She wore a green blanket around her entire body. The medical people had given her the blanket, and someone else had brought the food. Calls had gone out. Web had already talked to his stepfather. Everything seemed to have happened at once. He heard a television reporter was on his way to interview them.

Walter Eliot came back inside the room.

"They're getting ready to go," he said. "A tiny bit more light, is all."

"Cool," Web said.

Jill didn't say anything.

Web sucked his milk shake again. He had pushed it away, but he couldn't resist.

"They know the watershed," Walter said, taking a seat. "As soon as I started talking about it, they knew it. It's a wild river."

"Are they going back to Camp Lollipop?" Jill asked.

Walter shook his head.

"Not right away. Later they will. They want to get to the kids on the trail first."

"How are they going to find them?" Web asked.

"If the kids stayed next to the river, it won't be such a big deal. The rangers can buzz the river back and forth, and they can use a PA system to call to them. I'm pretty confident. Now that they know where they are, it should be fairly easy."

Jill went back to staring at the security window.

Web suddenly felt his stomach begin to rebel. He shifted on his seat, trying to predict what his stomach intended to do. He had eaten too much. He knew he was doing it as he did it, but he couldn't help it. The food had simply tasted too good.

"I'll be right back," he said and headed to the restroom.

As he hurried off, he heard the spark of a helicopter engine followed by the first slow churn of the propeller blade.

Titus shoved off from shore, the top portion of his body clinging to two pine logs lashed together like a boogie board. He wore his clothes, but kept his shoes tied to the top of the miniraft. It wasn't ideal. Nothing about the situation was ideal, and as he pushed off, he saw Paul and E staring at him, shaking their heads.

Titus wondered if he was missing the point.

He wondered if he was trying to be a hero.

He didn't think so. He hoped not. As the river began to gather him closer, pulling him gradually to the center, he played with settling himself higher on the pine logs. That had been the plan, the design. He had boogie-boarded plenty in both the Atlantic and Pacific, and he felt fairly confident he could handle the whitewater. It was simply surf, after all, surf that went on and on over rocks, with wicked cold water and deep dips that could sometimes swallow a raft.

Then, after another ten or fifteen yards, he had to stop thinking.

The first V – a wake formed from a rock in the streambed – came at him, and he swept down it, keeping his chest high on the pine logs. It wasn't bad. Not bad at all. He let his legs trail behind him, trying not to give them anything to brace against. He wanted to be a piece of kelp, a dangling, formless grass, the tail on a drifting kite.

But then the water started shattering.

It broke in every direction, swirling and biting, and he felt the logs begin to buck and dive, buck and dive, and he had to force himself higher on the boogie board to prevent it from rearing up and whacking him on the chin. He started to slip off it, and one of his shoes shot away. He tried to grab it as it drifted past him, but that was no use. The water pried him away from the logs. He made a fevered grab and caught the end, and something hit his knee incredibly hard. Then he went under, swirled once, and came up beside the boogie board. He lunged for it and felt one of his fingernails break off. Something struck his rib cage on the left side and he made a *hmmmummmpppp* sound that surprised him. It came out of his body without his cooperation, and suddenly he felt the cold digging into him, diving down toward his bones, and he tried again to snag the boogie board, but it had disappeared.

It had been a mistake.

He knew that clearly now.

E and Paul had been right. He should have gone back to Camp Lollipop and waited for fate to take a hand, but he had made this decision instead, thinking it the right thing to do, the *only* thing to do, and he had been wrong.

It was over for him, he thought. End of the line.

Then his knee hit something else below him, and the water suddenly gathered up into a white fist and punched him in the gut. It shoved him down, down, down, and the world became silent. His nose filled with water. He wasn't sure where up might be, and that had never happened to him, not even in some big California surf, but he remembered enough to wait and let the water release him. And it did. Then he was in a long section where the water ran like a tight piece of paper over a fairly shallow shelf of rocks and he tried to stand. But the water shoved him off his feet, and he felt himself trembling, trembling, and he saw pine trees and clouds above him. Crazy, crazy clouds that were moving faster than clouds would drift.

Hey, he said. But whether he said it aloud or not, he couldn't tell.

Then the water took him and tried to break his back on a rock, fixing him on a piece of granite, and for an instant he lay like a bug on a windshield, white, curling water splashing up and jamming itself into his mouth, and he almost let it finish him there. But he pushed off and rolled into a pocket of deeper water, and it was all cold, cold, cold.

And he wondered if the cloud had been a helicopter.

Wouldn't that be a kick in the pants? he thought.

Then a final wave came and chucked him end over end and his breath left him, and one of the logs from the raft came and gave him a karate chop on the shoulder. He figured that was probably it. He rolled onto his back and tried to keep his mouth out of the water for a second, but the water took him and pulled him down until he scraped the bottom of the river, and he thought, quietly, sedately, *Now I can rest. Now I can rest.*

CHAPTER 13

He was gone, just like that. E still couldn't believe it, even though she had witnessed it. Titus had climbed into the water, fallen forward, and hugged his ridiculous makeshift raft, then drifted away. It didn't seem possible. Something had to change. Something had to help fix what had happened. People didn't simply float away, not like this, not forever.

She screamed for Titus to come back. She screamed until she fell down on her knees and put her face in her hands.

"What were we thinking?!" she yelled through her fingers. "We are complete idiots!"

"He made up his own mind," Paul said beside her. "We couldn't talk him out of it."

"We should have tried harder! We should have insisted he come back with us. He's gone, don't you get it? We just watched the end of Titus."

"You don't know that," Paul yelled in response. It was like a roar, E thought. "Don't say that. You don't know that!"

"We should have gone with him, then. I can't believe this. I can't stand this!"

"Titus wanted to try it. He might make it. He really might."

E leaned over and thought she might be sick. She felt as though she needed to vomit, to get rid of every last particle of food or drink or anything that potentially brought comfort. How could they not have seen it more clearly? she wondered. That was puzzling, truly puzzling. You do not slip into a wild Arctic river with nothing ahead of you – no companions, no boat – and expect to live. It was insane even to consider such a plan, but they had let it go forward, weighing the pros and cons as if any part of it made sense. It was irrational behavior, nutty, stupid thinking, and her participation in it made her head hurt.

"If anyone can make it," Paul said more softly, "it's Titus."

"He *can't* make it, Paul," E said quietly. "Don't you see that? No one could. We were crazy to let him try it."

"We were desperate, that's all. Don't go changing the conversation now. Don't go reinventing things. We were desperate. We still are. Titus evaluated things and decided it was worth a try. He didn't do it lightly."

"But we shouldn't have let him try it at all," she said, slowly rising to her feet. "I can see that now. I don't know why I couldn't see it then."

Paul didn't say anything else. He walked over and squatted next to what was left of the fire. A little snow had begun to fall again, E noticed. The flakes came down independently, hardly bothering to collect into anything meaningful. The flakes seemed lost.

She went to join Paul by the smoldering fire. She squatted next to him, and her knees made an absurd *pop*. It made her think something had changed inside her, something had gone old and dead from the lack of nutrition.

"We should start back," Paul said. "If we walk hard, we can make it back in two days. Maybe less."

"And just leave Titus?"

"We can't join him, and we can't expect him back."

She threw twigs on the fire. Then she watched them slowly turn to flame. Paul threw some on, too. The smoke grew stronger.

"What should we say when we get back?" Paul asked. "How do we tell them about Titus?"

"We'll say he's traveling onward."

"You don't think we should tell them the truth?"

"It *is* the truth," she said. "It's the truth as far as we know it."

"We don't know he's dead."

"You're right, we don't."

"It might give everyone a little hope to think that Titus is heading to civilization."

"We can at least give them that," E said.

Then she stood, kicked some dirt over the fire, and started walking back to Camp Lollipop.

Titus crawled into the shallow water and rolled onto his back. He'd made it. He'd made it, he realized, but now he was going to die. He was exhausted and filled with water, and he wasn't positive, but he was fairly certain he had lost the matches. Not that they would be dry. Not that he could ever get a fire going, even if he had the strength to move.

But he had made it. He had made it down the rapids, and that was pretty good.

Pretty stupid, too, he realized.

It had been his one big mistake. After being fairly smart about things up until that point, he had chucked it all on one stupid decision. It was all okay, because the cold had started to do what not even the river had managed. He felt himself sinking away, melting like a quart of ice cream left out on the counter on a summer's day, like a ball of ice on a wool mitten when you hung it on a radiator.

The big shakes came next. When you lost your body heat, the big shakes rattled your ribs.

He tried to stand, but he couldn't. Something had broken down in his knee, and he knew he had some sort of cut on his head, up near the cowlick on the back of his scalp. He reached up and touched the injured spot, and his hand came away with blood. Blood diluted with river water. His teeth chattered like one of those toys you could buy in a cheap gag shop, the snappy jaws that jumped around and gnashed like a mouth gone nuts.

It would be over soon enough.

For the heck of it, he reached down into his shirt pocket and felt for the matches. He had trouble making his fingers work. They felt like chopsticks. But at least he hadn't lost the matches. That was something. And they were wrapped in plastic, so there was a chance, just a chance, that they might still work. Even if they did work, though, he didn't think he could get tinder and kindling and get a fire started. He needed a fire, for sure, but he was an amphibian, just crawling up out of the water, and a fire belonged to humans. He had centuries to go before he could harness fire.

Keep moving, he told himself. *Do anything.*

He tried to push up onto his knees, but he couldn't do it. Not at first. His clothes felt lined with ice. He counted to ten and tried again, and this time, at least, his body straightened out so that he was solidly perpendicular to the river. But his body had moved. So it was still possible to move, he realized. That was good to know. First his fingers had found the matches, and now his body followed his mental command. Not bad, he thought. Better than he had first imagined.

He pushed up again and this time managed to get to his hands and knees. His knee still flashed with pain, but he stayed in that position until his head cleared a little. When he felt more solid, he began to crawl.

He felt like a baby doing it, but it was safer than trying to stand. The ground was cold, he sensed, but really his body had gone colder than anything else around him. He felt the shakes starting deep in his core. He had to stop twice in his pitiful crawling to wait for them to stop. His knees hurt on the pebbles that covered the shoreline. His scalp throbbed, and he was sure it was still bleeding.

He picked up the first stick with his mouth. He did it without thinking. He did not trust himself to lift a hand away from the earth, so he did what a dog would do: He used his mouth. He carried the stick to a boulder where he might be out of the wind and dropped it there.

Fetch, he told himself.

It nearly made him laugh.

It took him fifteen minutes to round up enough small wood to have a prayer of lighting a fire. He made sure he had several pieces with dried lichen. They would burn, he knew, if he could get a match lit. He still didn't know if the matches worked, but that was out of his control. Either they would work, or they wouldn't. Meanwhile, you acted *as if.* He had learned that in Boy Scouts. Do your best, prepare, make good choices. Some of it, however, would always be out of your control. He couldn't know if the sulfur matches would be sufficiently dry to strike a spark. Out of his control now. He had simply to go along and do his best and meet opportunity halfway.

When he had his sticks together, he slowly moved into a sitting position, his back against the boulder. But as soon as he looked down at his wood, he realized he had a problem. He could not make his fingers work, so two issues presented themselves. First, he could not break up the wood so that it made a proper nest for the flames. The best he could do was to employ his fingers as dull rakes, and he did that, pushing the twigs together into something resembling a tepee. But the shakes kept erupting up from his core, so that he sometimes became distracted, fascinated by what was going on in his body. He was the reverse of a volcano, he reflected. A volcano spewed hot magma, but he, on the other hand, swallowed heat and turned it to ice.

The matches constituted the second issue.

He could not open the plastic bag to get them out. He could not hold a match to strike it. And he could not use his mouth, because if moisture from his lips touched the match heads, he would never be able to get them to ignite.

It was a pickle. He solved the first part of it by holding the plastic bag together with the heels of his hands while he ripped the plastic apart with his teeth. The matches fell onto his lap, which was not a good thing. When he tried to collect them, his stiff fingers and a round of the shakes made coordination impossible.

Almost, he thought. He had almost made it.

For a while he sat and closed his eyes. His mind felt empty. He fell asleep, he knew, because a few minutes later he woke with a jolt. He would die, he knew, if he didn't keep moving, and he wasn't quite ready for that to happen. He used the heels of his hands to trap a match and carry it to his mouth. It took him a long time to do it. When he had the match in his mouth, he pushed down onto the ground and tried to strike it against a rock.

To his astonishment, it flashed on the third try, a bright sulfur flash that stung his nostrils. Smoke blinded him and made him jerk his head to one side. The match went out in an instant. His lips felt warm from the effort.

So it could be done, he reflected. That was interesting. It could be done if he could move his mouth and lips into the proper position and manage to drop the match into the lichen. Yes, it was a decided long shot, but it was possible. If a thing is possible, then it's worth attempting.

He started the long process of moving a second match to his mouth. He closed his eyes when the shudders came fast and thunderous through his core. The lichen branches scattered at the jerking of his body. The matches glinted as they fell to the rocks, into a crevice down there, and he put his lips to the earth trying to find them.

△   △   △

In amazement, Paul watched the rescue guy rappel down the rope.

Paul's stomach did a flip-flop as he watched. Wind from the helicopter hit everything, bent the trees back, shoved the grass sideways, made the river water turn choppy and bright all at once.

E grabbed him and started to jump up and down.

Paul wanted to join her – they were saved, after all – but he couldn't feel it. He couldn't jump up and down and laugh and point to the rescue guy zipping down the rope beneath the helicopter. It was great to see the helicopter, of course, of course, of course, but did it have to show up an hour after Titus took to the water? Or a day and a night after Seldon had headed back to Camp Lollipop?

He felt angry. He pushed away from E and grabbed a rock off the shore, and for a second he wanted to chuck it at the guy coming down the rope.

It's not that easy, he thought.

You don't just fly in, string a rope to the ground, and zip down. It wasn't that easy. He felt his skin flush and his gut twist, and he felt as angry as he had ever felt in his life.

He turned and pegged the rock as hard as he could back toward the forest. Then he picked up another and did it again. He threw three more before he felt something begin to cave in inside him.

"Yeah, yeah, yeah!" E shouted.

She kept dancing and pointing and yelling.

He rubbed his sleeve against his eyes. Then the rescue guy stood next to them. His goggles made him look like an alien or a bug, and he shouted to ask how many?

How many what? Paul wanted to ask.

"Three people!" E shouted. "One of our people went down the river. Titus. His name is Titus."

"Down the river?" the guy asked, his voice lost a little as he turned his head to look at the rapids.

It was loud with the copter and the river.

"Just a while ago!" she screamed. "An hour, maybe longer."

So maybe she hadn't been jumping up and down with happiness, Paul realized. Maybe she was jumping up and down with anxiety over Titus. Paul felt something click inside him, and he comprehended the best way to help Titus was to tell the guy what he knew.

"He tried to swim the rapids because he thought we needed to get out. . . ."

The rescue guy cut him off and spoke into his shoulder. It was a radio, Paul understood, doubtless connected to the helicopter. A second later, the helicopter reeled in the rappelling line and shoved off like a dragonfly leaving a flower bud.

"They'll check the river," the rescue guy said. "You say he just tried to swim it?"

Paul nodded.

"A while ago. Where the river tightens between the walls of the mountains!" E said, shouting though it was no longer necessary to shout.

"And there's another guy," Paul said. "Seldon. He was on his way back to camp."

"Back toward the lake?"

"You know about the lake?" Paul asked.

Paul urged his mind to get with it, to make the connections it needed to make, but he was too tired to ask much more of it.

"We got everybody out of camp," the rescue guy said, pulling down his goggles so they hung on his neck. "Your dad, right? We got three out of camp. You say there's another person on the way back to camp?"

"He should be there by now," E said.

"Let's get you to sit down. The copter will be right back. They'll find him if he's there. The one in the water, I mean."

"He thought we had to make it out. Titus, I mean," Paul said.

"It's okay. Everything is okay now. You hungry? I've got some PowerBars in my vest. My name is Dan, by the way. Dan Kelly."

Paul didn't realize how exhausted he was until he had collapsed onto a piece of driftwood not far from the water's edge. It was over. It was over, but it was not over. The rescue guy handed them PowerBars, and Paul thought he had never tasted anything better. Or sweeter. It was coated with honey and some sort of flakes, and he had to concentrate to chew it. The rescue guy, Dan, squatted in front of them.

"You did a pretty great job surviving out here," he said. "You know, a lot of people wouldn't have made it this far."

"Some didn't," Paul said.

The man, Dan the man, nodded.

"How about Buford? Our dog?" E asked.

"Got him. He's okay. We've had a vet look him over. He's a little underfed, but he's okay."

"Good," E said.

She said it softly, almost like a prayer, Paul thought.

It would be over soon enough, Titus thought. The shakes came more rapidly now. Before he had experienced moments of composure when his body at least tried to follow his thoughts, but now that had all disappeared. He trembled when he wasn't shaking insanely. Pretty soon, he knew, his core would run out of heat once and for all, and the fire had been a good idea, but you needed fingers to make a fire and he no longer had real fingers. He had ice-cream-cone fingers. He had Popsicle fingers. He tasted sulfur on his tongue and lips.

An odd thing kept happening, though.

He couldn't help thinking about the strange cloud he had seen when he had been in the river. It had looked exactly like a helicopter, which was impossible, naturally. He was certain it was wishful thinking, that was all, but it had been convincing. Persuasive. He now sat against the boulder, facing the river, the matches scattered underneath him, and the peculiarly shaped cloud occupied his mind. Clouds could look like helicopters, he knew. They could look like anything. Who hadn't played the game of finding animal shapes in clouds? Or faces? He had wished for a helicopter, for rescue, but that was natural and easy to explain. Wishful thinking. He was like a cartoon character seeing an apple pie as a desert mirage when he was starving.

Then, out of the corner of his mind – Yes, minds had corners, wasn't that amazing? Wasn't that something to know? – he heard gravel crunch.

A bear, he thought.

He didn't mind a bear eating him. Not once he was dead. In fact, that was a pretty cool way to return back to the earth. But he didn't want a bear to get on him now, starting to lick him, huff his bear breath in his face, then slowly curl back his lips. That had to happen eventually. Eventually, the bear had to take a bite, just like you had to bite a sirloin finally, because you couldn't lick it forever.

"Hey," someone yelled. "Hey."

Titus tried to answer. But then more gravel crunched near his head and a woman looked down at him, a woman in a uniform, and the woman said over and over, "We got you. Titus, right? We got you."

"Yes," Titus said.

"You made it. What have you been doing? You trying to light a fire?"

He nodded. Or maybe he spoke. He couldn't be sure.

"Good man. Don't give up. Never give up."

He didn't say anything, though. He wasn't sure what question he answered or not. Or even if there had been a question.

"Yes," he said. "You got me."

SURVIVAL TIP #4

When returning from an extreme situation — like a severe period of isolation — learn to be patient with yourself. Just as it took time to acclimate to your former situation, it will also take time to adjust back into your life. Remember, things have changed not just for you, but for your family and friends as well. While you may understandably focus on what you have endured, your friends and family have experienced things as well. Take your time. Do not feel slighted if someone does not comprehend entirely what you have been through. Recall your feelings when someone showed you photos from a vacation they had recently enjoyed. Unless you were on the vacation with them, chances are you don't find it as interesting as they do. It may feel unfair that people don't "get" your situation. Take it easy. Go slow. Be gentle with yourself and others.

EPILOGUE

One bright, moonlit night in the beginning of November, a hunting party of wolves came out of the forest, crept along the banks of the lake, and spent nearly an hour searching for food. They did not rest or stop long at any one spot, but probed unfamiliar scents and moved with their back legs tensed and ready to carry them away. The wolves were gray-colored and matched the pale light from the moon. Only their eyes gave them away. When they turned their heads to look, or to peer more closely into the confines of the curious pine hut, the moon snapped against the surface of their eyes and went bright for a moment. It turned their sight to fire.

In that same hour, a horseshoe rabbit lay quivering beneath a thornbush on the outskirts of the wood. It watched the wolves move around the clearing, and it fought a dire impulse to flee for its life. Had any individual wolf come near, the rabbit would have panicked and succumbed to its elemental need for blind flight. Snow fell over the scene, and the rabbit, white in its winter coat, blended perfectly into the ground, a lump of beating blood in the otherwise empty snowscape.

Ice already trapped the fuselage of the plane that had brought *Junior Action News Team* to Camp Lollipop. It had been too late in the season to remove the plane body, though the insurance company had agreed reluctantly to see to it the next spring. The truth is, they would never carry out the task. The plane slid farther into the lake the following thaw, but in that first winter birds sometimes landed on the slick fuselage and preened in the dull sunlight. Now and then, a new swelling in the plane let water reach an untouched pocket of air, and at those times the plane would groan in a ghostly moan. It took seven seasons for the ice and water to claim the plane entirely. Web's nest floated for a long time in the last air pocket against the upper side of the fuselage, then, saturated at last, drifted to the bottom and lost all shape.

For a while, the crash site became an attraction. Pilots pointed it out to their passengers whenever they passed it, and snowmobilers searched on maps for its location. Eventually, however, people lost the thread of interest, and Camp Lollipop returned to its natural state.

The trees that had been sliced off at the top by the incoming plane never regained the height of the surrounding forest. The broken pine tops fell, one by one, until a person would have missed them unless she or he had known what to look for. In time, of course, those trees would fall and take all memory of the plane that had cut them off and bent their tops toward the lake.

One slightly miraculous thing occurred at the site, though no human witnessed it. It occurred before the plane slid entirely underwater, when a bear, swimming, felt something solid beneath its paws. Thinking it had come to nothing more than a boulder, it climbed onto the fuselage and stood for a moment in the late-summer sun. It was a young bear on the edge of its adulthood, and it stood for a moment enjoying the restful evening, the warmth brought by the sun. Light caught the last little surface of the plane's aluminum side and threw its reflection up into the air. Had anyone been there to see it, the bear would have looked mythical, lit by fire from below, its brown hair turned golden in that instant.

There was no way for that bear to know but, nearby in its grave six inches from the shoreline, the pilot's knife rested. Twice it was thrown up onto the shore by winter ice, then was pulled back into the water by the spring thaw. Its six-inch blade had rusted and turned to a brown color, not unlike the dull stones that covered the lake bottom and climbed onto the shore. Even in the harshest sunlight, it no longer glinted or tried to show itself. The leather wrapping around its handle had fallen away in small pieces. Mud sheathed it finally, and it sank down into the earth, never to be used by a human hand again.

No light. No air. No way out.

STAY ALIVE

C A V E - I N

Who will survive?

The floor began to heave and move and the walls, even these huge stone walls, she realized, had started to shake. It went on and on. Probably it was only a few seconds, but it felt like a million billion years, everything shaking and dancing, and for the tiniest instant she nearly convinced herself the wind had caused everything. Strong winds, very strong winds. But the shake came up from the ground, you felt it in your feet and in your guts, and the magazines were made of stone. Rock. Dirt. Wind couldn't do much to it.

Then everything became quiet. Supernaturally quiet. That was the strangest thing of all, she thought. She looked around, her headlamp catching the expressions of people near her. Some looked scared; others looked bewildered. Mr. O'Connell held his hands in front of him like a person walking down a dark hallway. And Bob Worm, the giant Bob Worm, had turned crazily into a karate stance, ready to combat whatever came at him. It made her smile to see him, because only Bob Worm would figure you could karate chop a tremor, and she kept her headlamp beam on him for a three count.

And then someone screamed.